The Holiday Experiment Files of the Sugimori Sisters

Brigid Collins

Frosty Owl Publishing

The Holiday Experiment Files of the Sugimori Sisters

Frosty Owl Publishing

Paperback:
ISBN: 979-8-89728-020-9

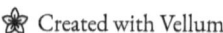 Created with Vellum

OTHER BOOKS BY BRIGID COLLINS

ACKNOWLEDGMENTS

Thank you to my father for being my guinea pig on these stories, and to my mother for making them shine with perfect grammar and punctuation. Any remaining errors are my own.

Thank you to my friends, Michael, Rob, Alex, and Clarence for all the lunches spent talking and commiserating about the business of writing.

ONE

The Dimension of Love

The moment Ellen Sugimori snapped awake on Friday the 13th of March, she was already a jumble of nerves. She lay curled in her bed, nestling under the thick blankets she'd piled on against the still-lingering chill, and wallowed.

The problem wasn't just that today was Friday the 13th. Ellen wasn't usually too superstitious, after all, and she could handle a bout of bad luck on most days. No, the problem she'd woken up to was one that she herself had sown the seeds for one month ago exactly.

Because on Friday the 13th of February—the last school day before Valentine's Day—she had put her heart on the line and secretly delivered a Valentine's chocolate to her chemistry lab partner, Krista Martin, the prettiest, smartest girl in Ellen's fifth-grade class, and one who seemed never to notice Ellen other than to ask her to pass the test tubes or hold the beaker steady. Ellen would give a lot to have Krista smile at her or, dare she hope, sit with her at lunch!

At the time, Ellen had thought the note she'd included was terribly clever. She didn't want to make her identity as Krista's secret admirer too obvious, but hopefully with the right hints, with the cute stickers of characters from Ellen's favorite manga series, *Neko Hime*, dancing on both the note and the box of chocolate, and with the careful explanation Ellen had penned of the Japanese holiday White Day—*it's the day when people who get Valentine's chocolate give return gifts, if they like the person!*—someone as whip-smart as Krista was could figure it out by the time White Day came around. Ellen had thought having a month to imagine how she'd react when she discovered Krista's return gift on White Day would be fun.

It turned out, the month had given her just enough to time to build her slight worry of *but what if she doesn't figure it out* into the deep, sickening dread of *what if she doesn't like me?*

Ellen's tummy burbled, and she let out a moan of misery and burrowed deeper into her blankets.

There was no help for it. She couldn't possibly go to school today. If she had to face her desk and find it completely empty of anything that could be a return gift, empty of even a note, she'd *die*.

On the other side of the bedroom, the rustle of clothes and muffled thump of schoolbooks hitting a messy bed signaled that Risako was already up and well on her way to being ready for school. Ellen peeked over the edge of her blankets to confirm this and met Risako's eye.

"Hey, lazybones," said Risako. "It's not often I get to bother *you* out of bed. Time to get up! Time for school!"

Ellen groaned and pulled the blankets over her head. Little Sister wouldn't understand. Not only was Risako entirely enamored with school and learning, as a first-grader, she couldn't possibly have anything so grown-up as an unrequited crush on one of her classmates.

"I'm not going," Ellen mumbled. "I'm sick."

Risako came over to Ellen's bed and lifted the edge of the blanket. "Really? You don't look sick. Unless... oh no! Ellen, you've caught Dorky-Sister-itis! It's fatal."

Not in the mood for sisterly teasing, Ellen growled and yanked the blanket out of Little Sister's hand. "My tummy hurts. I might throw up, and I'll be sure to do it all over your science experiments."

She looked pointedly at the table on the other side of the room, which was covered in Risako's many in-process cardboard machines. Those machines always managed to get both Risako and Ellen in trouble through whatever weird magic—though Risako insisted it was *science*—they worked on.

Risako huffed. "Like you don't mess my experiments up enough already. Fine, I'll go tell Mom you're playing sick."

"I'm not playing," Ellen said, but Little Sister was already out the bedroom door. Ellen pulled her blankets tighter around herself. She knew Little Sister wouldn't actually tattle on her, but the part of her that was already worrying about today's bad luck wouldn't let her relax fully.

Finally, Risako returned with Mom in tow. Mom immediately knelt by Ellen's bed and placed her cool hand against Ellen's forehead.

"You do feel a little warm," Mom said. "Risako said you thought you might throw up?"

If Ellen had to face Krista's rejection in front of their whole class, she definitely would throw up. "Yeah."

The concern on Mom's face made Ellen feel a little guilty, though.

"Eri-*chan*, I have to go to work today. Will you be okay here by yourself? I can have Mrs. Thomas next door come check on you."

Ellen nodded. She felt awful enough to keep up the pretense for their elderly neighbor.

Mom tucked the blankets more neatly around Ellen's shoulders, brought the trashcan closer to the bed, and kissed Ellen's forehead. "You get some rest, then. Come on, Risako. I'll call your sister in absent, and then I'll take you to school."

Risako followed Mom to the door, but she paused at the threshold and looked back at Ellen with narrowed eyes. "Have fun playing hooky, but don't touch any more of my experiments."

She left, and Ellen was alone with her broken heart and that cryptic remark.

Ellen stretched out under the blankets. She had no idea what had given Little Sister the idea that Ellen had been touching her things. The *last* thing Ellen wanted was to deal with the trouble any one of Risako's strange prototype cardboard machines caused. It was bad enough when Risako lassoed Ellen into poorly piloted flights to Mars or terrifying dives through shark-infested waters. Nothing would make Ellen tempt fate by messing with those machines without Little Sister there forcing her to do it!

And on Friday the 13th? No *way*.

The slam of the door downstairs told Ellen that Mom and Little Sister had left. She held her breath, listening for the rumble of Mom's car as it pulled out of the driveway, then the rev of its engine as they drove off.

She released her breath. She was alone, at home. She didn't have to face rejection of any kind today.

Instantly, she relaxed. Her anxious fear still thrummed in her heart, but it was dulled now. The danger had been put off for the whole weekend, at least. Suddenly, she felt pretty hungry. Bracing for the billow of chilly morning air, she flung the blankets off and then swung her legs over the side. Her thin pajamas left her shivering, but she giggled and grabbed her bathrobe from where it hung off the bedpost. She didn't even have to get dressed today, not if she didn't want to! She could lounge in her pajamas, snuggle up in her robe, and read *Neko Hime* all day.

She went down to the kitchen, made herself some rice, and drank a glass of orange juice. But as soon as her stomach was full, she regretted it. The gnawing worry over Krista's reaction surged to life now that it had food to writhe around, and Ellen was back to curling up and moaning.

She'd just about worked herself up to letting hot tears spill down her cheeks, imagining all the cruel ways Krista could fling Ellen's feelings back in her face, when something up in her bedroom *thump*ed.

Ellen went utterly still. The kitchen chair she sat on pressed painfully against her back and legs, but she didn't dare shift even a tiny bit. A heavy silence echoed through the house in the wake of that sound.

Then: a soft *shush*ing sound, like cardboard sliding against a wooden floor.

Ellen's already tormented heart leapt into her throat. Someone—or some*thing*—was up in her room, and it was touching Little Sister's experiments. The very same experiments Little Sister had warned Ellen away from, the ones Ellen had a vested interest in *not* triggering. And the only one home to deal with this intruder was Ellen.

What should she do? Calling the police came to mind, but then she might get in trouble for pretending to be sick. And besides, they'd laugh if she told them she was afraid that the intruder would trip one of her first-grader sister's science experiments.

Maybe, if Ellen could be sneaky and smart like Neko Hime on a mission, she could protect the science experiments and get whoever it was out of their bedroom.

Still, she snatched up a rolling pin before she crept up the stairs, taking careful steps to avoid making them creak.

Whatever it was in there was back to thumping. It sounded like heavy boxes full of pots and pans were being hefted onto the floor. A bump, as if someone had knocked against the table Little Sister used for her science work, and then the sliding hiss of the bag of pipe cleaners, construction paper, extra cardboard bits, and glitter Little Sister kept on hand falling open and spilling its contents.

Something yipped, and an odd snuffling, whimpering sound followed.

Ellen tightened her grip on the rolling pin.

Carefully, she leaned around the corner and looked at the intruder.

In the middle of the bedroom stood a creature on all fours, covered in white fur except for a pair of leathery black wings folded tightly against his back. His feet were scaled and clawed like a bird's feet, and a cluster of tailfeathers as white as the fur fanned out from his hindquarters. The creature was swinging his two-horned head from side to side over Little Sister's work-table, knocking cardboard constructions and unfinished pieces of experiments here and there.

Ellen couldn't help it. She screamed. But who could be stealthy when there was an actual *monster* in their bedroom?

At her scream, the monster whirled to face her and let out a shrill screech of his own. The sound was a mix between a hawk's cry and a big dog's startled baying. The monster thrashed backwards, his huge bat wings flapping, and he crashed into the table. What pieces of cardboard and in-process experiments hadn't already hit the floor went flying now.

The monster's face had a rather puppy-like look to it, with fluffy white fur curling along a—now that Ellen really looked at it—cute snout, with a pair of big, melted-chocolate brown eyes staring at her, wide with fear.

That was what broke through *Ellen's* fear. Now that she saw this intruder's face, he reminded her too much of Mrs. Thomas's little white terrier for her to keep being scared of him. Plus, the poor thing was clearly just as frightened of her as she had been of him!

"Hey, it's okay, I'm not gonna hurt you," she said, keeping her voice high just like she would when approaching a dog. Whatever this creature was, he was clearly lost.

And then he shocked her all over again by opening his mouth and speaking to her!

"Oh," he said, his tone mournful and watery. "Oh, no. I didn't think any of you stayed here during the daytime. I was being so careful, too, keeping out of sight until everyone left every day. Oh, no."

"Um," Ellen said. She would not scream again, there really wasn't any reason for it. "What are you even doing here?"

The monster flapped his wings again in agitation. "I didn't mean to! I just wanted to impress my boyfriend! I didn't think following the tiny-smooth-girl through her portal would bring me to *this* strange dimension! Now I'm trapped here, I can't figure out which of these weird boxes will get home, and even if I do, Thrrryk won't want to be my boyfriend anymore."

The monster wailed, a tearful mix of bird whistle and puppy whine.

Ellen tried to sort out what he had told her. This strange dimension? Doing tricks to impress a boyfriend? The tiny-smooth-girl? Considering the monster's furry, feathery exterior, Ellen supposed a human would look pretty smooth. And with the qualifier of tiny...

Put together, the pieces had Ellen's heart sinking. "Ugh. Little Sister's been working on some experiments, all right." Whatever it was Risako hadn't wanted her to touch, she'd apparently been testing it on her own, and had apparently brought along a stowaway. Ellen didn't know if she was angrier that Risako had built some new machine at all, or that Risako had gone testing it without Ellen around to keep an eye on her scientific antics.

On top of that, now this stowaway was *Ellen's* problem to deal with, and on Friday the 13th of all days.

Just like always, she thought, rolling her eyes.

Well, first things first, she needed to get her unexpected guest calmed down. It would be pretty awkward if the monster's loud crying brought Mrs. Thomas over to see what was going on in a house that was supposed to have only one sick girl in it.

"I'm Ellen," she said. She approached the monster and patted him on his fluffy white shoulder. "And I'll help you get home if I can."

The monster sniffed, and his wings drooped. At least they weren't flapping anymore, threatening to knock more things from Little Sister's table or Ellen's shelves.

"I'm Shyylk." The monster bobbed his head in greeting. "You are not the tiny-smooth-girl, but you live in this room with her, yes? You know which of these boxes will open the shiny door I followed the tiny-smooth-girl through?"

Ellen glanced at the scattered cardboard boxes. "Not a clue. But I might be able to figure something out if we sort through them together. We'll need to be careful, though. Some of my sister's experiments are... unstable."

This morning was certainly turning out far differently than Ellen had expected it would! When she'd woken up with her tummy writhing and her heart broken, she'd never have pictured herself kneeling on her bedroom floor beside Shyylk, and she definitely wouldn't have pictured herself willingly rifling through Little Sister's experiments! If she let herself think about the fact that she was *hoping* to find one that would open a portal to Shyylk's home dimension, she might faint from disbelief.

"Tell me about your boyfriend, Shyylk," she said as she inspected and rejected a long, thin box covered in bits of construction paper.

The monster puffed up in obvious pride. "Oh, Thrrryk is the smartest, handsomest one in our clan. His color is purple, so he is the sky to my clouds! He knows the names of every plant that grows in the Gyrating Forest, and he can catch a Rollybeast without breaking a tailfeather."

Ellen didn't know what any of those things were, but they sounded impressive, so she made a good show of *being* impressed. "He sounds like a wonderful boyfriend."

"He is," Shyylk said with a sigh. "He always makes certain to share his Rollybeast with me at lunch. Or, well, he did. But now I've gone and done something stupid, chasing the tiny-smooth-girl. I'm sure he won't want to eat with someone so unintelligent anymore."

His tailfeathers drooped, and the fur that had puffed in pride lay limp against his body.

Ellen wanted to comfort him and tell him that surely wouldn't be the case. But how could she do that, when she herself was absolutely certain that Krista would be utterly disgusted by the idea of eating lunch with Ellen?

"I know how you feel," she said instead. Her voice came out just as droopy as Shyylk's tailfeathers. "I told a girl at school that I like her, and now I'm so afraid she'll reject me that I couldn't go to school today. That's why I'm here."

Ellen and Shyylk both sighed as one, and silence fell. Ellen thought she'd never seen a more dejected pair than the two of them sitting with slumped shoulders and hanging heads among all of Little Sister's ridiculous cardboard boxes.

"Maybe I should just stay here, like you," Shyylk said. "I don't know if I can stand seeing Thrrryk's face when he tells me we're breaking up."

"Oh, no, you can't stay here. Not forever. You'd miss home too much. Remember the purple sky? And there aren't any Rollybeasts here. What will you eat?"

"The food in the cold-box downstairs hasn't been too bad," said Shyylk, but he sounded uncertain.

Ellen shook the mopey feeling off and reached for another cardboard box. "You can't hide from Thrrryk forever. Might as well see what he says when you get back, right? After all, he might be impressed!"

"Maybe. And you will probably need to return to school someday, yes? Maybe your girlfriend will like your note. Oh, what's that box you've got there? It looks like what the tiny-smooth-girl had."

Shyylk craned his neck to get a look around Ellen's shoulder, ignoring the way Ellen was spluttering that Krista wasn't her girlfriend. Eventually, Ellen gave up her denials and focused on the strange scientific device in her hands.

It was a box that had clearly held shoes at one point. The lid was taped in place, and a large rectangle had been cut from it and replaced with a sheet of plastic wrap revealing the inner workings of tangled pipe cleaners. At the top, the words DIMENSIONAL VIEW SCREEN had been written in pink crayon. To the left of the plastic wrap window was an old milk bottle cap with an arrow drawn on it. At the bottom, Little Sister had affixed a calculator with a mix of tape and glue, which made the whole contraption awkwardly weighted. Beside the calculator was another pink word: COORDINATES.

"Well," Ellen said, turning the box this way and that. "I never know how any of these crazy things will work, and most of them don't do what even Little Sister wants them to. But this sure *seems* like something that could open a portal to another dimension."

Now an entirely new source of dread churned at Ellen's tummy. Forget her fear of Krista's inevitable rejection. Without Little Sister here to explain this thing to her, how was Ellen supposed to know how to avoid winding up in a dimension full of starving T. rexes?

Shyylk seemed to pick up on her nerves. "Are we surrrre I can't stay here? I could live on cold-box food."

Ellen gave him her best Big-Sister scowl. "Shyylk, you have to be brave the way you were when you dove after my sister. I'm sure your bravery is one of the reasons Thrrryk became your boyfriend in the first place! Now, come on. We can figure this out together and get you home before Mrs. Thomas comes around."

She stood up, her knees shaking a little—she told herself it was from all the kneeling, not from fear—and raised the box she hoped would open a portal to Shyylk's home dimension.

To his credit, Shyylk stood up straight and puffed his chest fur up again. "That's right, I am brave, and Thrrryk knows it, even if it's only because I'm too stupid to know better."

"That's the spirit, I think," Ellen said, but she was distracted by the slip of paper that had come fluttering out of the box. Unfolding it revealed a sparse set of notes in Risako's handwriting.

"Dimensions I've been to," Ellen read. Five lines of numbers followed that. Under them was "HOME=4368." Then: "Chance of stowaways: possible???"

"I'd say: definite," said Shyylk.

Ellen scanned the list of numbers again, but she couldn't

figure out if any one in particular linked to Shyylk's home. She supposed she'd have to just pick one and find out. Making a decision, she punched some numbers into the calculator. "Now, uh, stand back."

She meant to twist the knob of the milk bottle cap, but before she could, the plastic wrap screen flared to life with an incredibly realistic image.

Strange trees like Ellen had never seen danced and twisted around each other on a field of yellow grass. Among the trunks, small round animals tumbled and rolled as if they were playing at being gymnasts. Over everything hung a wide expanse of purple sky.

"Home!" Shyylk trumpeted, sounding very like a parrot imitating a chihuahua. "That looks just like home."

"Wow, first try even," Ellen said. Usually these machines took a few attempts to hit the right coordinates. Now she turned the knob, and as she'd guessed, the machine truly engaged.

Where Little Sister's worktable and the pile of non-dimension-hopping cardboard used to be, a glowing, sparky portal now yawned, filling the bedroom with orange and blue light. Within the circle of the portal was the same image they'd seen on the screen, now accompanied by a smell like cinnamon and marshmallows.

"Home!" Shyylk repeated. His fur bristled, and he danced in place, his bird claws clicking on the floor. Then, before Ellen could make a single suggestion, he stepped through the portal.

Ellen sighed. She'd hoped to be able to take a moment to change into something besides her pajamas and bathrobe, but this *was* a Little Sister misadventure, even without Little Sister here. Comfort was not the priority.

She shoved the portal machine into the bathrobe's big

pocket, gathered the robe around herself, and followed Shyylk through the portal.

At once, she knew something was wrong.

The moving trees and rolling creatures that had looked so vibrant and lifelike through the screen and the portal suddenly took on a flat quality. It made Ellen feel strangely like she was about to lose her balance, and when she tried to wave her arms to steady herself, she found she couldn't quite do it. She glanced over at one arm and nearly gasped when she saw that it was as flat as a piece of paper!

The only reason she didn't gasp, she realized half a second later, was because her *lungs* were as flat as paper, too, as well as the rest of her.

"This...isn't...right," Shyylk wheezed beside her. He was looking like a stuffed animal that had lost its stuffing, flat and flappy. Somehow, he'd managed to wriggle over to where Ellen was about to topple over.

"It's...two...dimensional!" Ellen managed to gasp out. "Got...to...go...back."

Being entirely two-dimensional made fumbling the portal machine out from her pocket difficult. Her flat fingers kept missing the edges. Her lungs burned from lack of air.

Finally, she managed to get something of a grip on the machine. Carefully angling her fingers and ignoring her now very painful, very empty lungs, she typed in the number for HOME from Little Sister's list.

The portal opened, showing a view of the bedroom, and Ellen and Shyylk both waved and flapped their way slowly over the orange and blue glowing threshold.

When they both made it across, they lay on the floor gasping like fish.

"My home is definitely not two-dimensional," said Shyylk once he'd gotten enough breath to puff his chest out again.

"We're far too civilized to have fewer than four dimensions in *our*, uh, dimension."

"I believe you," Ellen said, rubbing her tummy. All that gasping had her feeling sick again.

"But after facing that, I think I feel more ready to deal with seeing Thrrryk again. He will definitely see how brave I am when I tell him how I survived being two-dimensional for a few minutes! Let's try another number."

Ellen got back to her feet, enjoyed the sensation of being perfectly stable on her two properly wide feet, and punched the next number into the calculator. Shyylk was right. Whatever came next, it couldn't be as bad as a place where she couldn't breathe.

The image on the screen didn't give them much to go on. The only detail it showed was a swath of purple. Perhaps it was rippling slightly?

"It is the sky!" Shyylk said. He gave a delighted whistle and turned in a circle, chasing his tail feathers. "The beautiful, beckoning purple sky of my home! Not this silly blue thing your dimension calls a sky."

"If it's the sky, I'll fall as soon as we go through. I haven't got any wings," Ellen said.

"True," said Shyylk. "You may ride on my back."

So Ellen clambered up to sit between Shyylk's leathery bat wings. It was like snuggling with a giant terrier, and she stifled the desire to giggle. She clung to the fur on his neck with one hand for stability, and held the portal machine tightly in the other hand.

"Thrrryk, I am on my way!"

With a lurch, Shyylk flung himself through the portal. The wind his speed created ruffled Ellen's hair and his fur. At first, Ellen shivered with the chill this wind created, but the moment they passed to the other side of the portal, her shivers turned to panting in the hottest heat she'd ever felt. Sudden sweat made keeping her grip on Shyylk's fur difficult, and when gravity kicked in, it came from the opposite direction than they'd expected.

They weren't soaring into a wide-open purple sky, they were diving straight into the heart of a volcano filled to the brim with burbling, burning purple *lava!* Smoke rose in curls from the surface, smelling of charred rock and hot metal.

"Pull up, pull up!" Ellen screamed.

Shyylk pumped his wings, and his muscles bunched with the effort. Ellen dug her knees into his sides to keep her seat and devoted both hands to keeping her grip on the portal machine. With the way sweat was pouring off her, she was in serious danger of dropping the precious machine into the lava pit. They'd be in big trouble if that happened. She didn't dare try to key in the HOME sequence until they were away from the immediate danger.

For a heart-stopping moment, it seemed as if they wouldn't be able to pull away in time. The bubbling purple liquid came closer and closer, while the heat rose until Ellen's pajamas were slicked to her skin with sweat. A smell of burning fur wafted on the next cloud of smoke.

Then, with a snap, Shyylk's wings caught an updraft, and they were rising up and out of the caldera, emerging into a green sky streaked with puffy pink clouds.

Ellen didn't waste another moment typing in the HOME sequence, and when the orange and blue portal opened in the air beside them, Shyylk banked through it in two smooth wingbeats.

Back in the bedroom, Ellen made a mental note to thank Mom for turning the heater off earlier this month.

"That was too close," she said, wiping sweat from her face. "You're very brave, Shyylk, and your flying is amazing, but let's try to be smarter about the next dimension. Thrrryk won't be able to be impressed if you come home too charred for him to recognize you."

"You're right. Next time, we will merely poke our head in to verify if the dimension is mine before jumping in."

Ellen glanced at the list of dimension numbers again. How much time did they have before Mrs. Thomas came to check on her? It wouldn't do to be off in another dimension when that happened.

"Let's get to the next one," she said, already putting the number into the calculator.

The view screen flickered, then showed another forest full of dancing trees and rolling creatures. Ellen thought it looked subtly different from the first one. She squinted. Did it look more three-dimensional than the last one?

Shyylk peered over her shoulder. "It looks right, anyway. But maybe it's another copy."

"Only one way to find out, I guess," Ellen said. She turned the knob, and once again, the blue and orange portal opened in the place where Little Sister's worktable stood.

Displaying great caution this time, Shyylk tiptoed to the portal and poked only the tip of his puppy-like nose into the other dimension. He sniffed. His tailfeathers waggled.

"It doesn't seem as flat as the last one. And I think I see the village! Why, yes, there are my neighbors, going to hunt Rolly-beasts in the Gyrating Forest. And—oh! Thrrryk! I see him! Oh, he is even more handsome than I remembered."

Shyylk's whole body was a wriggling mass of excitement now. But, as he exclaimed over his boyfriend, the wriggling slowed, until his shoulders, wings, and tail all drooped with all the dejection he'd worn when Ellen first found him.

"He really won't want to be my boyfriend anymore when he hears how very silly I've been with these portals," he said.

Ellen rolled her eyes. "Oh, no you don't. I didn't suffer being so flat I couldn't breathe and nearly getting cooked in purple lava just for you to chicken out now! Get in there and talk to him, you big bird-brain."

Stuffing the portal machine in her robe pocket again, she shoved at Shyylk's hindquarters. He struggled against her, but gave up soon enough.

On the other side of the portal, the world seemed safe enough, even with the weirdly moving trees and odd purple sky. Certainly, she could fill her lungs, and the temperature was more middle spring cool than molten lava boiling. Ellen thought it might be a nice place to live, provided the Rolly-beasts were tasty.

But she didn't have long to assess her surroundings, because a monster just like Shyylk in every way except for the striking purple color of his fur and feathers was stalking towards them, a snarl on his puppy-dog snout.

"Shyylk! Where in the world have you been? I've been worried sick about you."

Shyylk's fur flattened against his body, and he pulled his wings in tight. He hung his head like one of Ellen's classmates getting detention. He said something, but he mumbled so much Ellen couldn't make it out, and she didn't think the other monster heard him, either.

"Oh, for heaven's sake," she said. Was this how silly *she* seemed, hiding away at home, pretending to be sick just so she wouldn't have to face Krista? The other monster, Thrrryk, didn't even seem upset about anything other than the fact he'd been worried, which surely meant he still cared about Shyylk and wanted to continue being his boyfriend.

After all, Mom and Dad got mad at her and Little Sister when they'd gotten themselves into a place where they could be hurt, but it didn't mean their parents didn't love them anymore. Just the opposite.

Uncertain if she was more exasperated with Shyylk or herself, she stomped between the two monsters. "You must by Thrrryk. I'm Ellen, and I'm here to tell you how much Shyylk wants to impress you. He's made some silly decisions along the way, but he was also very brave in dealing with the consequences of those decisions. He even kept us from getting burnt up in a volcano with his quick flying instincts. Do you still want to eat lunch with him and be his boyfriend?"

While she was speaking, Shyylk frantically shook his head and made shushing gestures with his bird feet, but Thrrryk cocked his purple head as if he was confused.

"Of course I still want to be his boyfriend. That's why I'm so upset about him jumping into that strange ring after the tiny-smooth-girl! I'm not interested in a long-distance, trans-dimensional relationship here."

Shyylk's tailfeathers rose, and his melted-chocolate brown eyes grew wide. "Really? You still like me?"

"Don't tell me you built up a whole thing in your head of me breaking up with you," said Thrrryk with a fond, long-suffering look on his furry face. "That's not fair to either of us. You have to give me a chance to tell you how I feel before you go wallowing."

"I'm sorry, Thrrryk," said Shyylk. "But I'm so happy, too!"

The two monsters hugged, an awkward-looking tangle of bird feet and bat wings and bumping puppy snouts to Ellen's view. But they seemed happy enough, so happy that Ellen felt a tiny tingle of jealousy. She wished she could hug Krista like that.

But she tamped the tingle down. Thrrryk was right. It wasn't fair to assign her fears of rejection to Krista before she gave Krista a chance to tell her how she really felt. What if Krista *did* like her? She'd have wasted a day playing sick at home when she could have been having a good time at school with her... with her *girlfriend!*

Done with their hug, Shyylk and Thrrryk invited Ellen to stay for lunch. But much as Ellen would enjoy spending more time with her new friends and exploring their strange dimension, she had more important things to be doing.

"Mrs. Thomas will be by to check on me any minute, and besides, I have someone I really need to talk to."

Shyylk nodded wisely. "Yes, your girl at school. As someone who has a boyfriend, I can tell you that communication is very important in a relationship!"

Ellen stifled a smile, but she shared a secret look with Thrrryk. *Yes, I know he's a ridiculous monster*, said Thrrryk's expression, *but he's* my *ridiculous monster.*

Waving to her friends, Ellen pulled out the portal machine one last time, and typed in the number for HOME.

She had some planning to do.

Not a minute after Ellen got back into her room and changed out of her sweat-soaked pajamas and bathrobe, Mrs. Thomas came by, her little terrier wriggling under her arm. He'd been playing in the yard under Ellen's window, Mrs. Thomas explained. Ellen told her she was feeling much better, and that she felt silly for having stayed home.

She scratched the dog's fluffy white head before Mrs. Thomas left. Then she went to make herself some lunch. Hopping between dimensions really built up an appetite.

While she ate, she considered using the dimension hopper to find a way to get to school, but with the way her luck had been going on this Friday the 13th, it was too likely that a teacher would stow away with her back home, and *that* was almost as scary as nearly falling into an active volcano. No, she'd just have to wait until chemistry lab on Monday to talk to Krista.

She spent the rest of the afternoon tearing through pages and pages of notebook paper as she used the time to come up with an apology for Krista. She'd just settled on the simple lines 'I'm sorry I decided how you felt before you had a chance to tell me yourself' and 'I really like you, and I hope you like me, too,' when Little Sister arrived home from school.

"Hey, Ellen. How's your Dorky-Sister-itis going?"

"I seem to be making a full recovery," Ellen said. "By the way, I updated some of your notes on the dimension hopping machine. You might consider adding some descriptions to the coordinates, you know, especially the ones that go places that might be dangerous for humans. Oh, and stowaways are more than possible."

Risako let out an affronted squeak. "I *knew* you'd been touching my stuff! Ugh. Do you know how many delicate calibrations you might have ruined? Maybe I *won't* give you this note your classmate gave me."

Ellen's heart raced at that. "A note? From a classmate? Who?"

"I dunno. Some girl."

"If you give it to me, I'll introduce you to the new friends I made today. I'm sure you'll find them scientifically fascinating."

Little Sister chewed her lip, but the fire of scientific discovery shone in her eyes. "Fine. Here it is."

She fished a folded paper out of her school bag and thrust it at Ellen.

Ellen, with her heart in her throat, read her own name on the outside, written in Krista's familiar handwriting.

. . .

Ellen,

I'm sorry to hear you're sick today. I was hoping to see you in lab. Maybe, if you're better on Monday, we can have lunch together? I have something to give you for this cool Japanese holiday someone told me about.

From, your lab partner

The heart drawn at the end of the note made the one in Ellen's chest swell with happiness. Maybe Friday the 13th wasn't such an unlucky day after all, when it fell before White Day.

Two

The Haunting in the Library

E llen Sugimori trudged down the stairs, slouched into the kitchen, and dropped into one of the creaky wooden chairs around the dining table with a heavy sigh and much rubbing at her tired eyes. Another night filled with strange dreams and little sleep.

"*Ohayou,* Eri," said Mom from her place by the stove. She shot a worried glance over her shoulder as she stirred their breakfast. "Did you not sleep very well again?"

Ellen returned Mom's greeting with another sigh. "No. I keep having dreams about this dumb ghost story assignment."

It wasn't a dumb assignment, Ellen knew that, but she couldn't help feeling frustrated with it. Reading and writing were usually her best subjects, but when her teacher had assigned Ellen's sixth-grade class to write ghost stories in time for Halloween, Ellen's brain had turned as mushy as overcooked rice, and shivers had started running through her body. If there was one thing she was truly frightened of, it was ghosts. She had no logical reason to be afraid, of course. As Little Sister had told her many times before, there was no *scientific* evidence that ghosts existed. But those reassurances didn't convince Ellen's imagination any. The idea of a dead person with unfinished business was just *spooky*.

A week had already passed since the assignment had been given, and still Ellen hadn't managed to wring even the hint of an idea onto a page, not one that didn't make her want to run screaming, anyway.

And then the dreams had started. Losing sleep made coming up with ideas even harder.

And sighing had become half of Ellen's communication now. She sighed again and propped her forehead in her hands, elbows resting on the table.

"I just wish I was done with it already. I wish Halloween was over."

Mom gave the pan another stir. "I thought you liked Halloween. Trick-or-treating is fun, right?"

"Oh, Trick-or-treating is great. That's just a bunch of kids running around in costumes and getting candy. But the ghost stories..."

Ellen trailed off with a shudder. Then she sat back to lean bonelessly against the back of the chair. "Maybe I'll just have to fail this assignment. I can probably make up the lost points in extra credit." She didn't like that idea. She had a perfect record for turning her homework in on time. Ellen *liked* being a good student.

A plate clattered on the table in front of her, and wafts of steam carried the scents of pork belly, leek, rice, and egg into Ellen's face. Ellen sniffed in the aromas automatically and perked up. Mom's cooking would surely chase away any monster of the supernatural, it was so tasty.

Mom turned the stove burner to low so the rest would stay warm until Dad and Little Sister came down, then brought her own plate to the place next to Ellen. "Maybe you just need to get inspiration for a different type of ghost story. Your sister has been asking if she can go to the Spooky Storytime in the children's section at the library. They're going to be reading Halloween stories for the little kids, so they shouldn't be too scary. Why don't you take her and see if those stories can point you in a direction that works for you?"

Ellen chewed her mouthful of rice and egg and thought about it. It wasn't like she was doing anything else. Today was Saturday, Halloween was three days away, and with it, the due date for her uncooperative and frightening story. She'd already procrastinated by finishing all of her other homework early, and even if she did decide to blow the assignment off, she'd already read every volume of *Neko Hime,* her favorite manga series, three times each. Plus, she hadn't seen much of Little Sister since this assignment came in. Risako seemed to have been absorbed in some new experiment of her own that kept her making strange noises of frustration way past their bedtime. If Little Sister had gone on any of her crazy, unexplainable scientific adventures this past week, she hadn't included Ellen in them. Maybe a trip to the library would be a good way for both of them to clear their heads.

"Okay," Ellen said. "That sounds like fun."

"What sounds like fun?" said Risako as she tromped into the kitchen. Her face was as gray and saggy as Ellen's had felt before breakfast. "*Ohayou, kaa-san. Ohayou,* Ellen."

"*Ohayou*, Little Sister. Mom says you want to go to the Spooky Storytime. I'll take you, if you want," said Ellen. She scraped the last bite of pork and leeks from her plate and savored it. Mmm.

Risako brightened, a wide smile splitting her face and her

eyes sparkling, and Ellen's spirits rose seeing her sibling looking more like her usual excited self. "You'll take me? That's great! This is going to be a really important session for my research. The Storytime starts at lunchtime and runs all afternoon, so I've got enough time to get all my gear ready."

Little Sister began shoveling food into her mouth like she was starving. Ellen suppressed a laugh at the serious expression on Little Sister's face.

Mom didn't suppress her chuckle as she rose and collected her and Ellen's empty plates. "Have fun, girls. Just be home in time for dinner."

"We will," Ellen said. Even with a Little Sister as excitable as hers, getting home in time shouldn't be too hard to manage today. Ellen certainly had no intention of staying out past dark, not unless there was trick-or-treating to keep her out, and that wasn't for another three days yet!

"Your Halloween costume is cool. All the other kids will be jealous of it," Ellen said, turning her head to watch Little Sister as they walked to the library.

"Thank you!" Risako said. "But it's not a costume. It's my uniform. It has all the equipment I need for my latest experiment."

Risako was wearing an outfit that could only be a Mad Scientist's get-up. A large white lab coat covered her from shoulder to knee, with a thick black belt that held a pair of clear plastic chemistry goggles and a couple of empty and capped test tubes. Another pair of goggles had been pushed up onto her forehead, ready to fall into place over her eyes with a simple nod. She wore black rubber gloves, and her left wrist sported a kind of wrist bracer made of cardboard with squares and lines scribbled on it to look like buttons and dials. On her back, she'd strapped a pair of empty gallon milk jugs, coated on the inside with black paint. A gray rubber hose snaked from the nozzle of one tank, over her shoulder, and snapped into a hook sewn onto the front of her lab coat.

Ellen raised her eyebrows. "Well, whether it's a costume or a uniform, you clearly worked hard on it. Did you sew that hook on by yourself?"

"I did!" said Risako. She was skipping along beside Ellen now. "Well, Dad helped a *little*."

They were at the library steps now, and Ellen made Risako hold her hand as they climbed. The steps were all of red and brown brick, which was pretty, but they were too wide for six-year-olds to navigate easily. Even ten-year-old Ellen still had to place her feet carefully, and she wasn't even in costume. Or uniform.

But they made it up with no tripping, and as a brisk autumn wind sent dry leaves skittering over the bricks behind them, Ellen pulled the glass door open.

As always, the silence of the library fell over them the moment they stepped inside. Ellen remembered how she used to be scared of that silence when she was really little, but she'd long since outgrown that fear. Now she willingly climbed into the silence like it was a fort made with her favorite blanket. Ellen stood for a moment, eyes half-closed, drinking it in.

"Oh, look, they got the Haunted Section set up," said Risako.

Ellen came alert again and looked where Risako was pointing.

The bookshelves in the first area of the library were the fiction section for adults. Ellen had poked through them a little bit, but she hadn't tried to read more than a couple. She still preferred the stuff she could find in the children's section downstairs. But she knew enough of the layout up here to know that the shelves that had been transformed into the haunted house attraction for the older kids and teenagers belonged to the horror section.

Those shelves were blocked off with a fancy, but ancient-looking, velvet rope, and the entrance to the haunted maze was decorated to look like the moldy black siding of an old Victorian house. Wispy white strands of cotton stretched between the shelves to mimic spiderwebs, and shadowy figures lurked just on the edge of sight. Purple and green lights made the books cast twisted shadows.

A sign out front of the attraction directed library patrons to ask a librarian to fetch any books from the horror section for them.

Ellen shivered. The idea of ghosts, even pretend ones, taking up residence in her library made her distinctly uncomfortable. It made that silence into something more like how she used to think of it. At least the ghosts were sticking to the horror section. *She'd* never step foot in there, even without the creepy decorations.

"I wonder if we can get a peek inside," Risako mumbled, fingering the cardboard around her wrist.

"It doesn't start running until tomorrow," Ellen said. "And they don't open until after the library closes for normal hours, anyway." Thank goodness.

She ushered Little Sister towards the stairs that led to the children's section with a gentle push on her shoulders. Thankfully, Little Sister went without a fuss.

The children's section didn't hold the same reverent silence as upstairs, and the ringing of kids' laughter echoed up the stairwell as they descended. The kids weren't *loud,* though, just happy.

If the adult section had turned creepy with the season,

cheerful Halloween excitement had taken over down here. Everywhere Ellen looked she found pumpkins carved with laughing faces, big fuzzy spiders made of pipe cleaners and googly eyes, and, yes, even ghosts, cut from white construction paper and taped onto the walls and ends of the kid-height bookshelves. These ghosts didn't give Ellen the shivers, though. They all sported friendly smiles or held bags of candy.

"Where is the Spooky Storytime happening?" Ellen asked after a quick glance around didn't reveal a Storytime in progress.

"I dunno. Let's ask at the desk," said Risako.

There was always a friendly librarian at the desk in the children's section, and Ellen spent enough time here to be recognized by all of them. Today, a man named Daniel was there, smiling as he sorted through some books that had been returned.

"Hi, Daniel," Ellen said, using her most grown-up voice. "Can you tell us where the Spooky Storytime is? I'm taking my sister to listen."

Daniel's smile widened. "Ellen! And Risako, right? Wow, that's a great scientist costume."

"Thanks," Risako said. "It's not a costume, though."

Daniel nodded like he understood. "The Spooky Storytime is in the naptime room. The stories aren't *too* scary, but just in case someone does get scared, they can still enjoy the library even if they have to leave the room."

That seemed practical to Ellen. The naptime room was normally where the littlest kids were taken when they got too tired to stay in the main library. Ellen hadn't been in there for a long time, and neither had Risako.

She breathed a silent sigh of relief. The room was all done up in soothing colors with happy sleeping animals painted on the walls. That environment would surely help quell *any* hint of her fear of ghosts and let her focus on finally getting an idea for her dumb assignment story.

Risako looked a little disappointed, but she only shrugged and walked away from the desk.

"Thanks," Ellen said, turning to smile at Daniel.

But her eyes fell instead on a flicker of motion just behind his shoulder.

There, floating between the cart full of books to be re-shelved and the computer, was a transparent old woman, wearing a mournful look on her face and holding both hands out towards Ellen. She was tiny, frail-looking, but dressed as nicely as the ladies who worked this desk. She even had a little transparent white square pinned to her blouse, like a librarian nametag.

Ellen drew in a sharp gasp, but the scream she wanted to let out got stuck in her throat.

I can't scream in the library! They'll throw me out! But—But it's a ghost!

Daniel moved between Ellen and the ghost-woman, peering at her in concern. "Ellen? You okay?"

With effort, Ellen managed to unstick her throat. "I—I saw a—there's a—"

She pointed a trembling finger over his shoulder. Daniel's eyes widened, and he glanced back with a quick, mouse-like motion. Then he let out a chuckle.

"Good one, Ellen. You really got me going for a second there."

Ellen blinked. The transparent woman was nowhere to be seen. The only thing she was pointing at was one of the construction paper ghosts taped on the wall. This one was deco-rated to look exactly like a little old lady librarian.

Oh, man, I'm such an idiot, Ellen thought as she hastily covered her draining fear with a shaky smile. "Yep. Gotcha.

Anyway, I'd better catch up with Little Sister. You never know what an unchaperoned Mad Scientist might get up to."

These kiddie stories had better be full of jokes and cutesy things, she thought as she followed Risako's trail, *or I'll never come up with an idea for this dumb assignment!*

◈

Ellen had heard some adults say they were "of two minds" about some issue or other before, but it wasn't until she'd listened to three or four of the Spooky Storytime tales that she understood that phrase.

At least, she had two thoughts in her one mind. One thought was that she was enjoying the stories. They were fun and cute, and the other kids, Risako's age and younger, were having fun listening, too. But... the other thought was that the stories weren't really about ghosts. They were definitely a little spooky, but mostly they turned out to be jokes or pranks or misunderstandings between a couple of very much alive people, or animals.

She wasn't getting any ideas for her own ghost story. And what was worse, the more she thought about it, the less she wanted to just drop the assignment. She had a perfect turn-in record this year! She'd worked hard for it! The thought of missing this one assignment made her stomach twist.

A sigh filled the Storytime reader's dramatic pause, and for a moment, Ellen blushed, before she realized *she* had not been the one to make the sound.

Risako was sitting cross-legged beside her, her shoulder slumped, as she poked at the cardboard thing on her wrist. She looked distinctly like a bored scientist, and not at all as rapt as the other kids were.

Ellen tapped Little Sister's shoulder, and when their eyes

met, she jerked her thumb towards the door. Little Sister nodded, and the two of them made their exit.

"Risako, I'm sorry. I wanted to bring you to the Storytime so we could hang out together again, but I got too wrapped up in worrying about this dumb assignment to notice you were bored."

But Risako shook her head. "I wasn't bored so much as I was disappointed. I was really hoping that—well, that Spooky Storytime would help me help you. But I wasn't able to collect any of the data I needed."

Ellen blinked. "Help...me? With what?"

Risako blinked right back, then spread her arms and indicated her outfit. "Isn't it obvious?"

"Nnnno?"

"All this stuff I'm wearing is supposed to help me gather data about ghosts. There's no scientific proof on the books that ghosts exist, and of course nobody can prove that something *doesn't* exist, so I was hoping to gather data to prove they *do* exist, which would in turn let me gather data to figure out how to protect ourselves against them, if they really do mean us living people harm."

Ellen felt like she'd been hit with a thick book upside the head. "You want to prove ghosts exist to *help* me? Risako, I'm *scared* of ghosts!"

Holy mochi cakes, if Ellen had solid proof that ghosts were really *really* real, she'd be in an even stickier situation with her assignment!

"Did you listen to the second part? If I prove they exist, I can prove how to defend against them. Then you won't have to be scared, and you'll be able to get your assignment done in time so you won't break your turn-in streak."

Risako stepped closer to Ellen, who was still frozen in place unable to think of anything else to say, and grabbed her hands.

"Ellen, you've always helped me with my experiments, even when you didn't want to. I just want to show you how I appreciate your help, and the only way I could think of doing that would be to do an experiment for *you* this time."

"Oh," Ellen said. The fear trickled away under the hopeful look Little Sister was giving her. Risako could be a pain when she got caught up in the excitement of scientific discovery, but Ellen knew that her sister didn't mean to get them into trouble. It was nice to know Risako did pay attention to Ellen, too. And in this case, Risako's logic was sound, once Ellen really thought about it.

"I guess this experiment of yours could help me, then. Thank you for thinking of me, Little Sister."

If Little Sister could fashion one of her weird cardboard machines to ward Ellen from ghosts, Ellen wouldn't say no to that.

Risako grinned widely. "Great, then you'll come with me?" She started walking towards the stairs that would take them back up to the adult section, empty milk jugs thunking hollowly against her back.

"Uh, sure? Where?" Ellen asked, following.

"The Spooky Storytime was a dud, so we've got to go to the next best place to run into ghosts." Risako shot a shadowed look over her shoulder as she put her first foot on the stairs. "We've got to sneak into the Haunted Section!"

Ellen tried to pay attention to Little Sister's explanations of her various sensors and data-collectors, but it was hard when the idea of walking willingly into a den of ghosts was making her palms clammy and her heart pound.

But the two of them were currently standing against the

brick wall at the back side of the horror section, lurking just out of sight of any librarians who might be keeping watch. A gap in the Victorian manor siding around the shelves here was just big enough that two girls could squeeze through. Little Sister's rundown was the only thing that stood between Ellen and their entrance of the Haunted Section. Ellen figured she'd better pay attention.

"I've spent the last week making tests and preparing this equipment. This is the Ect-O-Meter, which will tell us when there's ghostly material nearby," Little Sister whispered, pointing to her cardboard wrist cuff. "And these goggles are calibrated to let us see frequencies of light where ghosts are visible, mostly in the infrared range. Here, I brought one for you, too."

Risako unhooked the extra pair of goggles from her belt and handed them to Ellen, who took them mechanically. A window high up at the top of the wall let in streams of golden, late afternoon autumn sunlight. Ellen blinked up at it wistfully.

"Are you paying attention, Ellen? This part's important."

"Sorry. I'm listening."

Risako shrugged her shoulders, making the milk jugs shift. "If we manage to track down a ghost, that's when I'll need your help with these. They're ghost canisters. I treated them with special material I discovered that ghosts can't pass through, so we'll be able to capture a ghost, bring it home with us, and study it."

Ellen felt like she'd been hit with an ice-cold water balloon. "Bring a ghost home? Into our *bedroom?*"

"Yep! That's the safest environment for doing tests. Now, when I give the signal, I'll need you to be ready with the cap, so once I've got the ghost stored in the canisters we can close the lid and the ghost won't be able to escape. You got that?"

Ellen was having trouble swallowing. "Uh..."

Risako nodded. "You got it. You can do this, Ellen. You

wouldn't be my big sister, otherwise." She flashed a big smile at Ellen.

Great, Ellen thought, grinding her teeth at Little Sister's manipulation. *Now I have to go through with this.*

Risako grabbed the edge of the Victorian manor siding and pulled it back. "Go on, I'll follow."

That cold, wet feeling hadn't left Ellen yet, but she knew she couldn't turn back now. Not only did she want to maintain her perfect turn-in record too badly, she also couldn't throw away the nice thing Risako was doing for her here.

She filled her lungs until she felt they were about to burst, then wriggled through the gap.

The inside of the Haunted Section wasn't as dark as she'd expected, and she found herself letting that held breath whoosh out of her in sudden relief. She almost laughed when she realized she'd been prepared for ghosts to attack her the moment she stepped into their domain! There was a smell, though, older and dustier than the rest of the library. It made Ellen's nose itch.

With a soft scrape of plastic on wood, Little Sister clambered in, too. "Okay, let's try and navigate to where the strongest readings are," she said, tapping at her wrist. She held her arm out straight in front of herself.

Ellen looked at the cuff. It didn't seem to be doing anything. "Huh. Looks like there aren't any ghosts here after all. I guess we should just go home."

"Oh, no you don't," said Little Sister, grabbing at Ellen's arm. "The Ect-O-Meter has a really short range. We're just not close enough, that's all. Let's move further in."

Stifling a groan, Ellen followed where Little Sister led. They walked slowly up the length of one aisle, pausing every few steps so Little Sister could tweak a dial or push a button on the Ect-O-Meter. With every stop, the shadows seemed to close in further, and that old, dusty smell got stronger.

Even though the Haunted Section attraction wasn't running right now, parts of the show were on a creepy sort of display. Pieces of scary costumes draped from the shelves, waiting for the actors who would wear them and swaying slightly in the circulating air-conditioning. A couple of times, either Risako or Ellen would accidentally trip one of the trick mechanisms, and a book would fall from the shelf either right behind or in front of them, landing with a thick thump on the carpet. Ellen jumped every time, and her shoulders crept up to hunch around her ears, but by the time they'd reached the end of the first aisle, there was still no reaction from the Ect-O-Meter.

It wasn't until they started down the third aisle that Ellen realized someone—or something—was following them.

"Risako! Did you hear that?" she hissed, grabbing Little Sister's lab coat sleeve.

"Hear what?" Risako said. She jabbed at her Ect-O-Meter again to no avail.

"The floor creaked on the other side of this shelf," Ellen whispered. "Like a footstep."

"Oh, no. Do you think a librarian saw us come in here?" Risako dropped her voice to a whisper now, too. "We can't leave before we pick up *something,* at least. Find a way to distract them, okay? I'll keep scanning further ahead."

"What?" Ellen said. "I'm not going over there by myself!"

"Well, someone has to, and I'm already busy."

Ellen was too keyed up from all the things that had made her jump in this stupid haunted house to be nice now. "I bet that Ect-O-Thing doesn't even work. We could be surrounded by ghosts right now, and it wouldn't even—"

Outside the Haunted Section, the library lights went out, plunging them into darkness so deep Ellen couldn't see Risako right in front of her.

The long, low creeeeaak of a floorboard sounded again, this time right on the other side of the bookshelf to Ellen's left.

Once again, the scream Ellen wanted to let out got stuck in her throat.

Just before Ellen's nerves could get the best of her, a flare of green light cut the darkness, blinking furiously.

It was the Ect-O-Meter!

Risako's face, lit by the flashing indicator, was a mask of fright as she met Ellen's eyes.

"I think," she said in a trembling voice, "that we're surrounded by ghosts right now."

"Ellen, stand up! Put your goggles on!"

Ellen, huddled with her face hidden against her knees and her arms wrapped over her head, ignored Little Sister's tugging. There were *ghosts* here, swirling among the books, whooshing overhead, and making the hair on the back of Ellen's neck stand up. They were going to... they were going to...

She suddenly realized she didn't know what it was ghosts were supposed to do to the living. But whatever it was, they were going to *get* her, and Little Sister, too. She was so scared she couldn't make herself move an inch.

Little Sister tugged at her sleeve again. "Come on, Ellen. Put on your goggles. You'll see it's not so bad. Remember when we used my time machine, and you faced off against a T. rex? Or what about when we crash-landed on Mars? You've been brave on lots of adventures so far."

"Those adventures weren't *haunted*," Ellen said. But she fumbled for the goggles Risako had given her and got them sort of into position. The elastic band was too small for her, and her hands were shaking too much to adjust it, so the heavy plastic pressed uncomfortably against her nose.

Slowly, she lifted her head.

Floating amongst the shelves full of horror books were a bunch of transparent people, each holding a book or two, and all looking startled or even annoyed at the intrusion of two little girls into their space.

"More little girls?" said one sepia woman dressed like she belonged in one of those old photos where people didn't smile. She peered down her nose at Risako. "Why can't they stay in the children's section?"

"It's almost Halloween. Perhaps they've come looking for stronger shivers than they can get from children's books," said a lavender man. He tried a grin that showed all of his teeth.

But something about his face and the tweed jacket he wore reminded Ellen of her reading teacher from last year, a clumsy man who always dropped his chalk and lost his page, and she found herself on the brink of laughter rather than screams.

Risako looked positively delighted. "Finally! Oh my gosh, this is so much better than I expected. If I can just tweak this... there!"

The sepia woman looked affronted. "What on the ghostly plane is *that?*"

Risako held her arm out. "I've made a small modification to my Ect-O-Meter. Now it should be able to collect data from you ghosts here in your natural habitat without me having to bring one of you home with me. That should put *your* mind at ease, right, Ellen?"

"I guess so," Ellen said. Now that her heart wasn't trying to climb out her throat, she could unfold herself from her defensive position on the floor. She got to her feet slowly, steadying herself against the bookshelf behind her.

The ghosts—and there were a lot of them—came drifting

closer to stare curiously at Risako's Ect-O-Meter. The light, which had changed from frantically flashing green to calmly pulsing yellow, seemed to hold them in a sort of trance. The smell of old dust got stronger.

Ellen watched them sway in a circle around Little Sister. They didn't seem to be about to make a grab for either Little Sister or Ellen, and even the sepia woman looked calm and happy to simply stare.

At first, Ellen watched closely, certain that these ghosts would—finally!—give her an idea for her assignment. After a while, though, watching a bunch of people sway and stare got kind of...boring. That wasn't something Ellen ever expected to say about a group of ghosts, but here she was. She was bored, her goggles were pressing against her nose so hard she was getting a headache, and on top of that, the darkness of the library was worrying her.

"Hey, Risako," she called. The ghosts had gathered quite thickly around Little Sister now, and their transparent "bodies" made the little scientist's form kind of blurry and faint. "I think the library must have closed. We promised Mom we'd be home in time for dinner, remember?"

"Uh, right," said Risako, sounding very distracted. "Just let me... I'm getting such good data here... Give me a minute..."

Ellen bit back a huff and waited another minute, then another, then another...

"Risako?" she called again.

"Just a minute," came the reply.

Ellen rolled her eyes. Wasn't that just like Little Sister? No matter what the experiment was, she *always* managed to get them into trouble, and Ellen was usually the one who had to clean up the mess with Mom and Dad.

Well, maybe this time Risako was going to have to deal with the consequences herself. If she wanted to stay behind in the

Haunted Section while Ellen marched right out, headed home, and told Mom exactly why they'd been late for dinner, she could just—

"Psst!"

Ellen jumped and whirled towards the new voice.

Another ghost peered around the end of the bookshelf. Unlike all the others gathered around Little Sister, who were all adults, this one was a little girl, not much older than Risako. She was small and pale, and she motioned with one thin arm for Ellen to come with her.

Ellen did follow, too curious to be afraid anymore. If the adults hadn't meant to scare her, surely this girl didn't, either.

Once Ellen rounded the corner into the next aisle over, the girl stopped and turned large, watery eyes on her.

"Please," she whispered. "You have to leave the Haunted Section while you still can. Otherwise you'll end up stuck here, like me."

Ellen's veins turned to ice. "Stuck?"

"I was supposed to be waiting for my grandma to come pick me up," said the girl, her eyes shimmering with unshed tears now. "But I got impatient and went exploring. I stumbled into this place, and the other ghosts, I thought they were being friendly to a little girl who was lost, but they did something to me. Now I can't walk beyond the shelves of the Haunted Section, no matter how hard I try."

She turned around and twisted her arms to try and point at something on her back. Ellen squinted, and managed to pick out a little square of white amongst all the girl's pale, transparent clothing. It looked like one of the stickers every library book had on its spine, declaring what section it belonged in.

"See?" said the girl. "They'll mark you and your sister, too, if you stay too long."

Ellen's fear had ramped all the way back up to where it was

when the Ect-O-Meter had first gone off, but instead of wanting to curl up into a protective ball, she burned with the need to go after Risako. Nobody, not even a ghost, was going to permanently shelve her Little Sister without going through Ellen first.

But she *was* scared. Her hands, even as she balled them into fists, shook, and her legs threatened to give out on her as she ran back around the shelf to the cluster of ghosts. And when she saw how tightly that cluster had clumped up around Risako while she was gone, she gasped in dismay.

Risako was barely visible now, but what Ellen could see made her heart plummet into her stomach. Risako was glowing with ghostly light that washed out the blinking of the Ect-O-Meter, her arms and legs dangling limply as she floated an inch above the carpet. Her eyes were wide and staring.

And little tendrils of *something* gauzy and white were flowing from Risako to the gathered ghosts.

"Risako!" Ellen shouted, dashing forward. "Can you hear me?"

Risako's head tilted towards Ellen a little, but she didn't seem to see her sister. "Data points..." she moaned. "Forming... hypothesis...fascinating."

"Risako!" Ellen cried. "Let go of her, you big jerks!"

"I don't know," said the sepia woman, her mouth curling in a wicked smile. "A Mad Scientist belongs in the Haunted Section, don't you think?"

"Most assuredly," said the lavender man. He reminded Ellen less of her silly reading teacher now and more of a principal ready to administer detention.

The little slip of ghostly white paper he held supported the image.

"No!" Desperate, Ellen plunged both arms into the mass of ghosts, reaching for Little Sister. Instantly, the coldest cold she'd ever felt engulfed her, and her teeth chattered painfully. It wasn't long before her arms were totally numb. No matter how she tried, she couldn't catch hold of Risako with her fingers feeling fat and clumsy.

Too soon, she was forced to pull back. But when she tried, she found herself stuck. With horror, she looked down at herself and saw that she, too, was glowing with the same ghostly light as Risako.

"Oh, no," she moaned, trying harder to pull away.

The lavender man flicked his wrist, and suddenly where only one slip had been, there were now two. "A Mad Scientist can't be without her trusty assistant, after all."

He leaned closer to Ellen, closer, closer...

Fear made Ellen's heart race, and all she could think of was getting away, getting somewhere the ghosts wouldn't be able to touch her.

A pale blur streaked between them, breaking the strange light holding Ellen and sending her stumbling backwards.

When she caught her balance, she saw the little ghost girl standing between her and the lavender man, arms spread to block him and the other ghosts from advancing on Ellen.

"Run!" said the ghost girl. "I can't hold them for long!"

So afraid she couldn't think straight, Ellen ran.

She ran past books and shelves, past fake cobwebs and mannequins waiting to scare teenagers tomorrow evening, past wisps of ghosts trying to grab at her.

Finally, after running hard enough her legs felt like jelly, she staggered out of the horror section, out past the fake Victorian manor siding, and into the main lobby area of the library. Her sides hurt, and tears blurred her vision.

The lights were out everywhere she looked, and real silence reigned. This wasn't the comforting silence of people keeping to themselves and trying not to disturb other library visitors. It wasn't the friendly quiet of librarians moving softly among the shelves, putting books away and gently shushing people.

This was the silence of an empty building. Nobody else was here.

Nobody except Risako, that was, and Ellen had just left her behind, stuck in the trance of the trap the ghosts had lured her into.

"Oh, no," Ellen whispered. She was shaking hard now, fear giving way to disgust at herself. How could she have left Little Sister like that? What would happen to Risako in there?

What would Mom say if Ellen had to tell her she'd lost Risako in the Haunted Section of the library? And when Risako had only been trying to help Ellen, too!

"Oh my gosh, I'm the worst big sister ever."

She had to go back in there. She *had* to. She had to face her fear and confront those ghosts, not for the sake of her dumb assignment, but to rescue her sister.

But...

But if she went back in there, she'd only fall right into the same trap, and then they'd both be stuck just like that little girl ghost. That wouldn't help anybody.

Ellen shivered and wrapped her arms around herself. If only someone were still in the building, someone who could help her. She glanced around without really thinking about it, full of false hope.

But her gaze landed on the sign propped right at the front of the Haunted Section attraction.

ASK A LIBRARIAN TO FETCH ANY BOOKS YOU WANT FROM THE HORROR SECTION! THEY CAN GET IN AND OUT BEFORE THEY CAN SAY "BOO!"

"Before they can say "boo," huh? As if the librarians themselves were ghosts."

The moment she said it, her memory flashed back to her

encounter with Daniel at the librarian's desk in the children's section, and the ghost she'd seen down there, a woman dressed like the other lady librarians Ellen knew, wearing a name tag...

Instantly, all Ellen's fear transformed into urgency, and she ran through the lobby to clatter down the stairs leading to the children's section. The library might be closed, and all the *living* librarians might have gone home, but a *ghost* librarian...

Ellen's skin tingled at the thought of asking a ghost for help, but she shoved the feeling to the back of her mind and focused on not tripping down the stairs.

She crashed to the bottom of the stairs, thundered over to the desk, and was so elated to lay eyes on the ghostly woman floating at the cart of books there that she let out a whoop of triumph.

The ghost librarian lady looked up at her approach, startled, then wore an expression of such joy that the last dregs of Ellen's fear evaporated. The lady didn't look mournful, as she'd thought when she saw her earlier, just a little lonely.

"Why, my dear, whatever are you doing here at this hour? Not that I'm sad to see you. There have been precious few children coming to ask for my help since I took over the night shift," said the lady. She looked a bit sad at that, but her eyes sparkled with tears of happiness.

Ellen leaned far over the desk to pant out her request. "Please, I need your help. My sister got trapped in the Haunted Section, and the ghosts there are going to try and shelve her with them so she can't ever get out! But the sign said I should ask a librarian to fetch what I need from that section. So, will you?"

The librarian looked shocked. "What on the ghostly plane was your sister doing in there? That section is supposed to be off-limits to children your age, you know."

Ellen sniffed. "She... she was trying to help me get over my fears, but I got too scared and ran off without her. Please, she's a good girl, really! She just gets excited when she gets an idea for a new experiment. Even if she *is* a Mad Scientist, she doesn't deserve to be permanently shelved in the Haunted Section!"

Ellen blinked furiously, but she couldn't stop the tears from finally spilling over. What if this ghost librarian turned out to be just as treacherous as the others? They'd seemed friendly enough at first, after all. They were proving that all of Ellen's fears had been justified all along.

But then there was the ghost girl, who had only helped Ellen by warning her in time to run away. Maybe not all ghosts were so scary.

"Oh, you poor thing, don't cry," said the librarian, floating through the desk to pat Ellen on the shoulder. The touch was chilly, but it didn't make Ellen shiver like the others had. Instead, the cool sensation soothed her, and with a last sniff, she managed to stop crying.

"Come on, child," said the librarian, smiling. "I'll fetch your sister, and she'll be none the worse for her encounter with the ghostly plane. You'll see."

She floated up the stairs, and Ellen followed. Together, the ghost and the girl approached the Haunted Section.

Ellen waited, fear and impatience mingling within her, while the librarian floated through the entrance. Would they be in time? Had Risako already become one of the ghostly inhabitants of the Haunted Section? Ellen vowed, here and now, that if that was the case, she'd brave her fears every day to come see Little Sister.

A sound like a scuffle echoed out from the shelves, followed by a low moan and the slam of a book being closed.

Then a pair of shadows detached from the deeper darkness, and the librarian was back, Little Sister in tow!

"Risako!" Ellen cried, and flung herself at her sister. "Oh,

I'm so happy I don't have to come to this horrible place to visit you from now on."

"It's not so bad in there," Little Sister said, her voice muffled against Ellen's shoulder as she returned the tight hug. "There's some good books with interesting ideas on those shelves, you know."

Ellen pushed away so she could look Risako over. Her sister seemed as alive and excitable as ever, though there was something a little wispy about her edges. But the longer Ellen held her, the more that effect disappeared. "I think I'll stick to the children's section for a while longer, myself."

Risako sighed. "Ellen, I'm sorry. I wanted to help you, but you ended up getting scared anyway."

Ellen shook her head. "No, I'm sorry. No matter how scared I was, I shouldn't have left you."

"Ah, it's okay. I mean, all the data I collected turned out to be bogus, but I can always try again when I've had more time to prepare."

"Oh, Risako. Never change."

The girls hugged each other again, both squeezing so tight they had to gasp for breath.

"Oh," said the librarian ghost with a light sniff. "You two are such cute sisters. You remind me of my granddaughter, especially you, young scientist. She was always so eager to explore new places. But I didn't come in time to pick her up when she joined the ghostly plane, and I lost her."

She sniffed again, and pulled a ghostly handkerchief from her sleeve to dab at her eyes.

Ellen gasped. "The little ghost girl who helped me!"

Just then, the ghost canisters on Risako's back shook. Risako shrugged out of the arm straps, and with a quick twist, pulled the cap off the hose that snaked over her shoulder. A cloud of pale mist gushed from the hose, and a moment later, there stood the ghost girl.

"Grandma!" she cried.

The librarian gasped. "Clara!"

Risako grinned. "She helped me get away from those ghosts in there and asked me to carry her out in the canisters. She thought it would be the only way she could get past the bounds of the Haunted Section, and then she could go looking for her grandma."

Ellen's heart, so full of fear earlier, now swelled with happiness as she watched the two ghosts embrace one another. Before today, she'd never thought she could be *happy* for ghosts.

"Thank you, both of you, for helping me," she said when the ghosts pulled apart. "I think I can finally stop being afraid of ghosts. You're all just lonely, aren't you?"

"We were," said the ghost girl. "But we're not anymore."

She held her grandma's hand, and with a smile, the two of them faded out of sight.

"Wow," said Risako. "That was really nice."

Ellen nodded. Then she jumped, startled.

"Hey, the lights are on! When did that happen?"

The two of them looked around and were astonished to realize that daylight still shone outside. It was the orange-pink daylight of early evening, but still daylight. All around them, people moved about the library, trying to be quiet and studious. Pages turned, books slid onto shelves, people whispered together as they worked.

"We...didn't stay after closing?" Ellen suggested.

Risako looked just as bewildered as Ellen, perhaps even more so in her Mad Scientist costume. Uniform. "I guess we aren't late for dinner, then!"

Ellen shook her head. Had any of that ghost stuff actually happened? Or had her imagination run away with her? She tried to hold onto the memories, tried to picture the happiness of the little ghost girl and her librarian grandmother, but the harder she tried the more the images dissolved like smoke.

Finally, she gave up. "Let's go home, Little Sister. I feel like it's been a long day, and I *still* have to come up with an idea for this ghost story assignment, somehow."

She turned to head for the front doors and those too-wide brick steps, but Little Sister stopped her.

"What's this?"

Ellen looked where she pointed. Lying on the floor, right where Ellen thought she remembered the little ghost girl standing, was a book. Risako bent to pick it up, scanned the title, and handed it to Ellen.

"How to Write Ghost Stories, by Clara J. Hauntsford," she read out loud.

"Hey, I bet that could really help you, right?" said Little Sister. "Maybe I managed to give you a hand even if my experiment was a bust."

Ellen wrapped an arm around Little Sister's shoulders and steered her towards the checkout desk. "I think so. And maybe, once I finally finish this dumb assignment, we can work together to come up with a better experiment so you can get good data this time, okay?"

Risako smiled up at her, and Ellen grinned right back.

As she slipped her newly borrowed library book into her bag, Ellen yawned. She got the feeling that her sleep tonight was, for the first time in a week, going to be completely, totally, dreamless.

Unless, of course, she got so excited by her new ghost story idea that she stayed up all night to finish writing it!

THREE

The Santa Experiment

A soft thump woke Ellen Sugimori from her light sleep, and, seeing as it was Christmas Eve, she couldn't help the flutter of excitement in her heart at that sound. For that first sleep-addled moment, she allowed herself to wonder if Santa Claus had landed on their roof.

But she was too old to believe in Santa anymore. Any sixth grader who still believed that kids' story found themselves sitting alone at lunch more often than not. More likely, the thump had been Ellen's parents setting things up downstairs for tomorrow morning. Little Sister still believed, which was fine for a first grader.

Satisfied with that explanation, Ellen rolled onto her side to try to go back to sleep.

The soft thump came again, accompanied by the distinctive click of the bedroom window latch being flicked open.

Ellen sat up, throwing the covers off and opening her eyes

wide to try to make out the dark shapes of the bedroom. The long dresser opposite her bed, the closet door to her left slightly ajar, the slant of the ceiling towards the window. Light flooded in from the window, because someone had pulled the curtain back. Nothing so magical as silvery moonlight; it was only the regular orange glow of the streetlight right outside their house. The orange light fell over the small figure standing at the window, highlighting the fluffy fur-lined hood of a parka and a coil of thin rope slung over a shoulder.

Ellen blinked to make sure the sleep wasn't blurring her vision. "Little Sister, what are you doing?"

Little Sister let out a gasp that sounded suspiciously like "yeep!" and turned around. "Ellen! I thought you were asleep."

"Hard to sleep on Christmas Eve," Ellen said. She was coming more fully awake now, and her internal alarm system was clanging at her. The Risako-is-about-to-get-us-into-big-trouble sensors had picked up some major readings.

Risako shuffled beside the window, looking a little like she was doing the pee dance. "I didn't mean to wake you. I just have to go check on an experiment I set up earlier, then I'll come back to bed."

Ellen scowled and got out of bed. She shivered in the cold air as she crossed to stand in front of her irritating sibling. "No. Christmas is no time for science. It's all about magic and miracles and unexplained phenomenons."

Little Sister gave her a skeptical look. "It's 'phenomena.' And tonight is the only night I can do this experiment. I can't exactly prove whether reindeer can really fly or not without a so-called flying reindeer coming around."

Ellen groaned. "Risako. I'm not letting you sit on our roof all night waiting to see if Santa comes around. You'll freeze to death, and Mom and Dad will ground me for a week, at least."

"Oh! I'm not sitting out there all night. That would be

really inefficient. I set up a reindeer trap earlier. I'm just going to check if I caught anything. I thought I heard something clopping around up there a little bit ago, so I think something must have tripped it."

Risako turned back to the window and pushed it open. Cold air rushed into their bedroom, and Ellen's teeth were chattering in no time.

"Risako!"

But Little Sister had already swung one leg over the window sill, sending little clumps of snow tumbling in to dampen the carpet. Their window opened out onto the lower part of the roof, and it didn't take much in the way of acrobatics to get out there. Their parents had expressly forbidden such excursions, but though Ellen had done her best to follow the rules, they hadn't stopped Risako from setting up a number of sketchy experiments up there. Risako was nothing if not devoted to scientific progress.

Risako smiled back at Ellen and hauled herself the rest of the way out. "I'll be right back. Won't take more than a minute to check my trap."

Ellen stood there, seething, wrapping her arms around herself, and shivering in the frigid air pouring in through the window. She ought to just close that window right up, see how Little Sister dealt with being trapped outside the house all night in the snow. Serve her right for breaking the rules, and on Christmas Eve of all days.

But she knew she couldn't do that. She'd get in trouble, of course, but she was old enough to know right from wrong without needing the incentive of punishment to drive her decisions.

"Ugh," she said, and turned to tiptoe angrily through the house to grab her own coat and boots.

After a brief struggle to get herself out the window—she

was out of practice—Ellen clambered up the slope of the roof, going on all fours to keep her balance. Little Sister was crouched at the peak of the roof, prodding at an overturned cardboard box against the chimney.

Ellen groaned at the sight of the box, and her internal alarm system went off again. This was what she had been afraid of.

Risako's cardboard creations were the things that got them in the worst trouble, the trouble their parents didn't know about. Ellen didn't know how the machines worked, but they always seemed to do exactly what Risako said they would, from the rocket ship that actually took them into space to the time machine that flung them back millions of years. Somehow, it was always up to Ellen to get them out of whatever scientific scrapes Risako's prototypes got them into.

Ellen had no interest in crash-landing on Mars or running from a hungry T-rex tonight.

"Whatever's in that box, Risako, you'd better let it out and just come back inside," she said as she reached the top of the roof.

There probably wasn't anything inside it, of course. Now that she was up close, she saw the box wasn't nearly big enough to have caught a reindeer. It was only a normal printer paper box.

Risako prodded the box again. The box wiggled. A soft squeak came from inside.

Ellen's heart dropped into her tummy. "It's probably a squirrel."

Risako twitched her shoulder to let the coil of rope slide to her hand, and then started to lift the box. She hunched over it so Ellen couldn't see what she'd caught.

There was a sudden flurry of activity. Risako brought the box up and snapped her arm out to throw the rope over whatever it was. The squeaking sound came again, and the furious jingling of little bells. The box fell to the side and slid all the way down to the gutter, leaving a squared-off trail in the snow.

Finally, struggling to keep hold of her prize, Risako turned around. Her breath hung in big clouds around her head, and her cheeks were flushed with exertion.

In her hands, she held what looked like a tiny woman with rosy cheeks and shiny yellow hair, like a doll come to life. The ropes were wrapped around the tiny woman's torso, holding her arms tight against her sides. She was squirming and letting out high-pitched grunts as she fought in vain to break free.

"Oh my gosh," said Little Sister, her voice full of wonder. "It's one of Santa's elves."

Anger flared in Ellen's chest, leaving no room for her own wonder to blossom. *Great,* she thought. *Let's prove Santa Claus exists by kidnapping one of his elves.* That *won't get us on the naughty list.*

"You put that poor girl down right now, Risako. You're hurting her."

Risako glared up at Ellen. "I am not. And this is such a huge opportunity to do some research. It's even better than a reindeer. I thought I'd have to wait until next year to study the toy-making capabilities of Santa's elves."

She scooted around Ellen on the roof and slid down to their bedroom window, holding the unfortunate elf against her chest.

Ellen clenched her fists hard enough she felt the nails bite into her palms even through her mittens. She took her own seated slide back to the window and scrambled inside. She tried to keep any more snow from falling in with her, but gave up when she saw how much Risako had knocked in. The carpet was well on its way to being soaked.

Add another tally to the list of upcoming punishments, Ellen thought.

But she wasn't worried about what Mom would say about

the wet patch on their carpet, or even about what Dad would say when he saw their telltale footprints in the snow on the roof tomorrow morning.

She had a much bigger problem to worry about just now.

Little Sister stood in their closet, holding the elf against her chest with one arm as she dug around in the mess of things the two of them had shoved in there the last time Mom had made them clean their room. The elf's squeaks were muffled against the fluff of Little Sister's parka.

"Hold...still..." Risako grunted.

Then she let out a sound of triumph, and dragged something out into the patch of orange light from the window. It was the old glass tank they'd kept a series of doomed fish in a few years ago, scrubbed clean of algae and packed with all the extra colored gravel and plastic plants they no longer had a use for, but couldn't quite bring themselves to throw away yet. It still smelled a little bit like pond water.

Risako set about pulling the plastic plants out of the tank. "Shut the window, Ellen. She's squirming a lot, and I don't want her to get out if I lose my grip on her."

Ellen crossed her arms over her chest. "I will not. You let her go, or I will tell Mom."

Risako rolled her eyes. "I'm not trying to break the magic of Christmas, Ellen, but there's just so many things about the whole operation that haven't got explanations. If I can be the first one to figure out the key to Santa's single-night globe-trotting, I'll be in the running for a Nobel Prize for sure. That's not even touching how he can shrink to fit through a chimney, or the related technology of eating so many cookies and not gaining any weight."

Ellen gaped, and Risako took advantage of her silence to stuff the thrashing elf into the now-empty fish tank. She closed the ventilated plastic lid with a snap.

Finally, Ellen found her voice. "You're being bad, Risako. No, worse, you're being *naughty*. You're...you're *committing a crime!*"

Risako looked taken aback, and she rose to her full height, which was just to Ellen's chin. "I am not."

"You are, too. First, you were going to pull a grand theft reindeer. It would have been one thing if you just wanted to catch a wild reindeer, but Santa's reindeer are his property, so that would have been stealing. Now you're up to kidnapping. This poor elf is a *person*, Risako, and you just put her in a cage!"

Risako's eyes goggled out, and it was her turn to gape. Slowly, she looked back down at the elf she'd stuck in the fish tank. The little woman's face was red, her festive clothing rumpled, the jingle bells on her toes drooping. She was working at the ropes still, but not making much progress. Apparently, Risako had been paying attention on knot day in girl scouts.

"I didn't think of it like that," Risako said. Her voice had turned watery. "I just wanted to collect some data. Will they... will they send me to jail?"

The look of orange dismay on Little Sister's face melted Ellen's anger away. Well, most of it, anyway. As far as she could tell, they were still in big trouble. She sighed. "I don't know. If you let the elf go back home to the North Pole, probably not."

Risako frowned, but nodded.

As Risako knelt to open the fish tank, Ellen let herself breathe freely again. She'd worried that Little Sister would be too wrapped up in scientific discovery to listen to reason. That happened sometimes. That happened a lot, actually.

The plastic lid snapped off, and Risako reached into the tank. Then she let out a yip and yanked her hand back, shaking it.

"She bit me!"

"I don't blame her," Ellen said, coming to kneel by the tank herself. She reached her own mittened hands in and gently lifted the elf woman out. She set her on the carpet, then took the mittens off to pick at the knot. The elf smelled like peppermint. "Aren't you going to apologize, Risako?"

Risako chewed on her lip, still shaking her bitten hand. "Sorry," she eventually said.

Ellen rolled her eyes. "Good enough, I guess."

She finally got the knot to come loose, and the rope fell away from the elf. Instead of bolting for the window, as Ellen had expected, the elf just stood there, looking back and forth between Ellen and Risako.

Ellen picked the elf up and carried her to the window. She set her on the window sill and pointed up at the night sky where, just vaguely through the orange screen of the streetlight, they could see the twinkling of a few stars.

"There you go," Ellen said. "You're free to go. Use your magic to go back home, okay? And Risako really is sorry. She just gets excited sometimes."

The elf blinked up at her. Ellen made a "go on" motion with both hands. She wished she'd put the mittens back on. Her hands were getting chapped in the cold, dry air.

The elf shook her head, looking just like a lost little girl.

"Oh, no," Ellen groaned. "Risako, she doesn't know the way back."

"Oh, no," Risako parroted. "She has to go back. I don't want to go to jail!"

That last was said in a tone dangerously close to a wail, and Ellen shushed her. The last thing they needed was to wake their parents up now. "I won't let them send you to jail. But we have to think of something quick."

Risako's eyes lit up. "We could mail her to the North Pole! Kids send letters all the time, so the mailperson obviously knows how to get there."

"I'm pretty sure mailing a person is against the law, too," Ellen said. A look of horror had crossed the little elf woman's face at the suggestion.

"Oh. Well, hmm. Maybe we could... Or maybe... Oh, no. We're going to have to..."

She trailed off, and Ellen tapped her foot. "Spit it out, Risako. We don't exactly have a whole lot of time here."

"I know, but...you're not going to like it."

Ellen sighed, picked the elf up and let her sit on her shoulder, then closed the window. The relative increase in temperature was nice, at least.

"All right," she said, turning to frown at Little Sister once more. "Which of your prototypes are we going to have to use this time?"

"This is the Polar Exploration Vehicle, designed to make use of Santa-travel technology," said Risako, looking far prouder than she ought to after having committed a kidnapping.

The garage smelled like gasoline and road salt. It was also frigid. Ellen wished she'd taken the time to put on real pants instead of keeping her thin pajama bottoms.

Little Sister seemed not to feel the cold as she showed Ellen her latest contraption of scientific mayhem.

"It's really not ready yet. I wasn't expecting to use it until next year. The data I wanted from my reindeer experiment would have made it much more stable."

It was a sled, one of those long plastic ones that looks like an open kayak. Over top of the place a rider would sit, she had attached a hood of cardboard. The hood was fashioned to look like the body of a car, with a windshield cut out of the front. Through this windshield, Ellen could see a number of buttons and dials drawn onto the inner panels with different colors of crayon.

Ellen squinted at it.

"Isn't this top part...your rocket ship?" There was no way, no how that Ellen would go to space tonight. Not even to keep Little Sister out of jail. "I thought you were modifying that to go beyond the asteroid belt."

But Risako shook her head. "It's only based on that design. I figured my first test of it would be to go explore glaciers or something. I kind of thought of the North Pole as a distant goalpost. Like, real distant."

Ellen rubbed her arms. "Great."

"But it's the only thing I've got that might be able to get us to the North Pole, if the guesswork data I put into it works the way I hypothesized. Unless, of course, you'd rather try the time machine. I might be able to get that to take us to a place as well as a time, but I haven't been able to make much progress with its coordinate input system since, um, that one time..."

Ellen shuddered. "No, not the time machine. I guess we'll give this Polar Exploration Vehicle a whirl, then."

Working together, they got the garage open manually with what Ellen hoped was a minimum of rattling. Then they dragged the PEV out into the driveway. The orange light from the streetlight lay over the blanket of snow, making it look like fool's gold. It was quiet out here this late at night. Even the usual rumble of traffic on the interstate seemed softer than usual.

"We haven't got much time. Let's hurry," she said.

The elf woman, still sitting on Ellen's shoulder and wafting her peppermint smell under Ellen's nose, tangled her tiny fingers in Ellen's hair.

Risako climbed into the PEV, and Ellen carefully did the

same. Being larger than Little Sister, she couldn't help bending the cardboard a bit as she got in.

"Make bigger openings," she said in response to Little Sister's glare.

While Risako made preparations in the pilot's seat, Ellen settled into the spot behind her. She transferred the elf woman to her lap. It would be much safer than the perch on her shoulder, if the PEV lurched the way the rocket ship had.

Seconds passed, then minutes. Ellen was shivering hard now, but the PEV had yet to even twitch. It was, as far as Ellen could tell, nothing more than what it seemed: a child's sled with a hunk of cardboard taped on top of it. "Is there a problem?"

A frustrated grumble was all she got in response.

Ellen bit her lip. In her lap, the elf woman twisted to peer up at her with questioning eyes. Ellen shrugged, not wanting to disturb Little Sister's attempts to get her machine working.

After another few tries, Little Sister punched the drawn-on dashboard hard enough to dent the cardboard. Then she crossed her arms and huffed out a misty cloud. "It won't work at all. I just tested the engine two days ago!"

Ellen's heart sank. If they couldn't get this thing working, they had no chance of getting the elf back to the North Pole before they were found out. "Is there enough fuel in the tank?"

"Of course there is," Risako snapped. She pointed at the fuel guage, but Ellen saw only a scribbled rectangle marked as "full." She couldn't quite put her finger on whatever it was that was missing here, but the PEV just didn't have that special spark that made Risako's other machines more than the sum of their parts.

The elf woman crawled out of Ellen's lap and over Risako's leg to reach under the dashboard. The two girls watched as the elf touched crayon squares seemingly at random. After the third button, a loud beep sounded, making all three of them jump.

"What was that?" Ellen asked, rubbing her ears.

"I don't know. Hey, don't touch that. You'll mess everything—"

"SANTA-TRAVEL SYSTEM ENGAGING," said a deafening computer voice.

The PEV didn't just lurch, it zoomed out of the driveway at a speed that left Ellen's stomach back in front of the garage. At the bottom of the driveway, it made a hard left turn. Ellen and Little Sister both were slammed against the side of the hood from the force.

They were both screaming and flailing their arms all around the cramped space, but the elf woman sat up front, perched in the cut-out space of the front window, looking remarkably like the toy elf Mom had placed on the mantelpiece between Ellen's and Risako's stockings. She even wore the same smug smile as she watched the sisters freaking out.

"SANTA-TRAVEL SYSTEM PREPARING FOR JUMP," shouted the computer.

The PEV picked up speed as they zipped along their neighborhood street. Ellen realized they were headed not for the road that would lead out of the neighborhood, but for the cul-de-sac that was completely ringed with houses.

"We're going to crash!" she yelled.

Sure enough, the dark shape of a house loomed ahead.

Ellen squeezed her eyes shut and held onto Risako's waist. If they survived this, she swore she'd never get into another of Risako's untested machines again.

Multicolored lights flared all around the PEV. Ellen opened her eyes in time to see the elf woman touch another crayon button.

The house they were about to crash into suddenly jumped to the right, giving them clear access to the open field behind it. The colored lights stretched out into the field, becoming a tunnel of aurora borealis. There was a smell of hot plastic and gingerbread.

"JUMP ENGAGED."

Then the snow skimmer was going even faster, faster than sound, faster than *light*, surely, though even Ellen knew that wasn't possible.

In front of her, Risako was making a loud sound, which Ellen at first thought was a scream of terror, but soon realized was laughter.

"Oh my gosh, it's working! Just wait until we share this with the world. I'm going to be so famous!"

Ellen didn't say anything. She was too busy trying not to be sick. She didn't know how much more of this high-speed travel she could take.

All at once, the aurora lights stopped. In their place came a blurred landscape of ice and darkness. They were skimming along a snowfield far wider than the one behind their neighbor's house, and in the rapidly diminishing distance was a brightly glowing point on the horizon. A little village in the snow, Ellen thought.

The gingerbread smell was stronger now, along with the scent of peppermint. The air here was much crisper than it had been at home. Crisper, and clearer. Even at this high speed, Ellen could make out a thousand times more individual stars overhead than she ever had at home.

"JUMP COMPLETE. NOW APPROACHING DESTI-NATION: THE NORTH POLE. PRESENT DELIVERY SYSTEM INITIATING."

They were nearly upon the village now, but their speed hadn't dropped much. Were the snow-frosted houses going to jump out of their way like their neighbor's had? Or was this the point where Ellen and Risako were doomed to meet their messy ends, splattered against the red brick wall of the factory building?

In the open windshield, the little elf woman was grinning.

Ellen's heart jumped into her throat. "Risako, do something!"

Risako reached out and pressed a bunch of buttons at once. There was a screeching, glitch beep, and the PEV, now hurtling under an archway made of candy cane, began to fishtail. Risako pushed more buttons.

There was a bump. The elf woman was knocked down from her perch in the windshield and sent sprawling into Risako's lap. The PEV was now completely sideways. Ellen watched, powerless, as they careened towards the center of a little plaza, where a large and very solid-looking statue of Santa Claus stood.

With a crunch of crumpling cardboard, they struck the base of the statue and came to a jolting halt. Ellen's head was spinning, her vision all spotty. There was a hissing and ticking sound, like an overheated engine cooling down. The smell of cookies and melting plastic was overwhelming.

Risako groaned. "Everyone okay? I couldn't control it there at the end."

Ellen shook her head to get the spots out of her eyes. "You didn't have control of it at all."

Before either of them had a chance to clamber out of the wreckage, the cardboard hood flew open, and they found themselves ejected from their seats. Ellen landed in a pile of snow, which promptly began to soak through her pajama pants.

"PRESENT DELIVERY COMPLETED. MERRY CHRISTMAS. MERRY CHRISTMAS. MERRY CHRISTMAS. AND A HAPPY NEW YEARRRRR."

Ellen struggled out of the snow drift. The PEV was a smoldering mess at the base of the Santa statue. A dark coil of smoke rose from the cockpit to circle Santa's head like an ugly, oily wreath.

Ellen reached for Risako, who had landed nearby and was moaning as she sat up.

"I think it still needs some work," Risako said faintly.

"Where's the little elf?" Ellen asked.

Footsteps crunched through the snow, and an elderly woman's voice called out to them.

"Stay right where you are, thieves. I don't know how you managed to avoid the naughty list this year, but I'll rectify that before you can say 'Santa Claus is coming to town.'"

Ellen looked up to see a woman in a red dress and white apron advancing on them from the well-lit porch of the largest house on the square. On her shoulder was the little elf woman Risako had captured. Her arms were crossed, and her face was screwed up in a tiny scowl. The jingle bells on her toes rang angrily.

"How did she get over there?" Ellen asked. Hadn't the elf been shot from the PEV alongside the two of them?

Mrs. Claus—who else could it be?—clucked at them. "You stole my patented Santa-travel technology, and don't even know how it works? Typical unimaginative crooks. And Minnie here says you tried to *kidnap* her!"

Ellen shook her head slowly. Her vision was still dancing with spots. "Risako knows she was wrong to do that. She said she was sorry. And she didn't steal the Santa-travel tech, she just guessed at how it would work, right, Risako?"

But Risako averted her eyes and mumbled something inaudible.

"What was that, young lady?" said Mrs. Claus.

"I might have picked up a piece of hardware from Santa's sleigh last year."

Ellen's jaw dropped. "Risako!"

"My prototype wasn't working!" Risako said. "I just needed a little bit of help, you know, like a nudge in the right direction. I wasn't going to steal it completely. But then I couldn't figure out how to make my own technology work with what I'd taken from the Santa tech, and I knew I needed more pieces."

"So you resorted to kidnapping to get at them, I see," said Mrs. Claus. "I'm disappointed in you, Risako. I thought a fellow scientist would understand the value of doing your own work. What's more, you show so much promise! I've been watching your progress as you develop your prototypes. It took me centuries to develop a stable version of the Santa-travel system, but if you'd kept up your own work on the concept, you'd have gotten there in a few more iterations. As it stands, I'm afraid I'm going to have to put you on the Permanent Naughty List, along with all the other mad scientists."

She reached down and clamped a hand over Risako's and Ellen's wrists to drag them to their feet. "Come along, then. We'll carry out your sentences and have everything managed before Santa returns."

Ellen almost cried out how that wasn't fair, *she* hadn't participated in the kidnapping, and certainly not in last year's theft. But she held her tongue. Her brain had chosen to run through her memories of all the tiny crimes she'd committed throughout the year. All the extra snacks she'd snuck and hadn't shared with Risako, all the times she'd said she'd finished her homework when she really had a math problem or two left to solve. All the times she should have been keeping a firmer hand on Risako's more...dangerous experiments.

For instance, she could have kept Risako from breaking the "don't go out on the roof" rule. That would have stopped this whole fiasco.

But she could be better than that next year. Did she really

deserve to go on the Permanent Naughty List, with no opportunity for a second chance?

Did Risako? She was just a kid, only in first grade. Had she really used up all of her chances already, even if she had gone out on the roof when she knew she wasn't supposed to?

"Wait, Mrs. Claus," Ellen said. She had to clear her throat to keep her voice from squeaking.

Mrs. Claus peered down at her. "Yes?"

"What if Risako gives back the technology she stole? I mean, we came here in order to get this elf back home. Doesn't that, I dunno, count for something?"

Mrs. Claus stopped their forward march. They had reached the cozy porch of the large house. Cheery firelight flickered in the windows, and warmth billowed from the open door, but it all only served to remind Ellen of the soggy and freezing cold state of her pajama pants. She had never felt so nauseated by the aroma of holly and cocoa.

Mrs. Claus didn't let go of either of the sisters, but she did bend her knees so she was on a level with them. She turned her sharp gaze on Risako. "Is what your sister says true? Did you come to the North Pole purely to return Minnie?"

Ellen held her breath. *Please, Risako, say you didn't come to steal more Santa tech.*

"Well... I won't say I didn't think about the opportunity I'd have if we really made it here. That would be lying. So maybe I really should go on the Permanent Naughty List."

Ellen couldn't stop her moan of disappointment.

But Mrs. Claus laughed. "Honesty is admirable, especially when you're being honest about your crimes. And you did bring Minnie back, regardless of any ulterior motives you might have had. I was worried sick when Santa called and said she was missing."

Here she tipped her head towards the little elf woman, who

curled her fingers in Mrs. Claus's gray hair and gave it an affectionate tug.

"The truth, if we're being honest," said Mrs. Claus, "is that the idea of putting such a brilliant young mind on the Permanent Naughty List upsets me terribly. I'd hate to deny you the chemistry sets and robot kits and such that will come to you in future Christmas presents. I think, in light of your honesty just now, as well as your use of what you stole to bring little Minnie back home, *and* the fact that your sister is looking out for you, we can administer a somewhat lighter sentence."

Mrs. Claus released their arms, and Ellen and Risako exchanged wondering glances.

"Oh, thank you, Mrs. Claus. Thank you so much," Ellen said. "Risako will be good from now on, I promise. I won't let her go out on the roof anymore, either."

"I should hope not! Now, what we'll do is this: Risako will go on the regular naughty list for next year, and I will confiscate the, ah, Polar Exploration Vehicle and all the Santa-travel technology involved."

Ellen glanced back at the wreckage. A number of elves had appeared and were swarming over it, putting out the fire that had created that oily smoke and clearing away the crumpled bits of cardboard.

She looked back at Mrs. Claus. "Uh, how will we get home then?"

"I'll send you straight back using my own Santa-travel system, of course!"

Risako was very excited by this, and though she tried to be somber as she took her punishment, she couldn't seem to help herself from peppering Mrs. Claus with questions. Ellen, not nearly the scientist Little Sister was, couldn't follow the conversation. Besides, she was so tired after all this mayhem. It was almost Christmas morning, and they'd been out most of the night. Her eyelids began to droop, and she yawned more and more, until finally, as Mrs. Claus directed them into a pair of horizontal travel pods, she couldn't keep her eyes open any longer.

~

A soft thump woke Ellen from her light sleep. It was Christmas morning, and wintery sunlight and cold air streamed in through the open... window...

She sat bolt upright, throwing the covers off and scrambling out of bed. The window was open, and Risako was sitting in it, straddling the window sill. Her fluffy parka whispered as she raised her arms to hold something up.

"Risako, how could you?" Ellen hissed.

Risako turned, and Ellen saw she held a pair of binoculars. "What? I'm not going out on the roof again, don't worry. I just wanted to see if I could make out hoof prints on everyone else's roofs. A good reindeer print would go a long way to proving that reindeer can fly, don't you think?"

Ellen blinked. "I guess so."

Had last night's adventure really happened? She didn't feel like she'd been anywhere other than her bed. And when she poked her head out the window, there were no footprints— reindeer or little girl—on their own roof that she could see. There wasn't even a damp patch on the carpet.

Although that would change if Risako didn't get back inside soon. "Come on, Little Sister. Mom will ground us both if we ruin the carpet in here. Let's go see what Santa brought for us."

"Sure," said Risako, sounding distracted. She took another look through her binoculars, then lowered them and shook her head. "I just don't know how he does it all in one night. It calls for more data, that's for sure. Maybe I could set up a reindeer trap next year…"

"Oh, no," said Ellen, pulling Little Sister back inside and closing the window. "Definitely no reindeer traps."

Christmas, Ellen had decided, was no time for science.

FOUR

The Most Perfect Party Ever

Ellen Sugimori's arms ached under the strain of two overfilled shopping bags. Her cheeks were cold and her nose was running, a discomfort made all the worse for being unable to wipe at it with her arms full. Even worse, the sidewalk was covered in treacherous patches of snow and ice, and her boots were pinching her toes.

She wasn't exactly happy with her purchases, but the supplies she'd picked up were the best the party store two blocks away from her house had in stock. If she was going to throw the most perfect New Year's party for the kids of her parents' friends tonight, she needed to start somewhere.

Still, for all her current frustration, throbbing muscles, and frozen-numb skin, she wasn't regretting agreeing to help her parents out this year. It would be the first time she would be allowed to stay up until midnight. More important, Krista

Martin, the prettiest girl in Ellen's sixth-grade class, would be coming to this party.

Most important, Krista Martin kissing Ellen at midnight.

But that last could only happen if everything, absolutely everything, about this party was perfect, right down to the last seconds.

It *had* to be perfect.

Tummy butterflies at the thought of her crush gave her a burst of energy. She hefted her bags to get a better hold on them, swiped her nose on the puffy purple shoulder of her coat, and tromped through the last snowdrifts leading to her front door.

Still, once she tumbled into the warmth of home, let her burdens slide to the floor, and replaced her too-tight boots with her comfy house slippers, she heaved a giant sigh of relief.

The Christmas decorations were still up in the living room, and the air smelled piney. The afternoon daylight streamed in through the front window, making the carefully cleaned and arranged furniture appear to glow. All that was left to do before the party tonight was to set up the snack tables, hang some of what Mom called "elegant decorations," and welcome all their guests in.

At least, that was the case here, in the room where the grown-up party would be held. Ellen's tummy butterflies withered into tummy grasshoppers at the thought of *her* party space down in the basement. She had so much work to do.

But Ellen was old enough to know sitting and fretting over her work wouldn't get it done. She took another deep breath of Christmas scent—for fortification—then bent to pick up all her shopping bags again.

A loud thump sounded from upstairs. It was followed by a sharp crash, a moment of heavy silence in which Ellen's heart had time to sink into the midst of the leaping grasshoppers. Then:

"I've *done* it!"

Little Sister's shout of victory had a definite ring of science to it. Ellen should know. She'd been through enough of Risako's experiments, both successes and failures. (Ha! They were mostly failures.) Too many, if she were honest, though she always strove to be a good, supportive big sister.

The rapid *thmp-thmp-thmp* of Risako's house slippers preceded her appearance on the stairs.

"Good, you're home. I mean, I knew you were home. I've *fixed* it!"

Ellen blinked up at Little Sister. She was wearing her usual science outfit of white lab coat and goggles that made her eyes look as round and protuberant as a dragonfly's. A pair of rubber gloves went up to her elbows, and they squeaked against the banister as she gripped it to lean over it and stare down at Ellen. Her smile was so wide her cheeks looked ready to jump into orbit.

Ellen sighed. She knew the "good big sister" thing would be to ask Risako what she'd fixed. But her Perfect Party To-Do List still felt like a mountain of homework looming over her. "Good for you. Does that mean you can help me carry these things downstairs? I have to set up everything, and I'm running out of time."

"Didn't you hear me? I said I fixed it."

"I heard you," Ellen said, tugging on her shopping bags. How had they gotten so much heavier since she'd put them down?

"So you can do the party set up later. Come on!"

"Little Sister, one thing you learn when you get older is 'never put off to tomorrow what you really super have to do today, especially if you want the girl you like to kiss you at midnight.'"

Little Sister wrinkled her nose. "Eww, kissing."

Ellen ignored her. With a groan, she got the bags back off the floor. Now to lug the things allll the way to the basement stairs. Then down them.

She practiced some quick breathing techniques.

"Ellen, you've got all the time in the world for that! Even if you *are* gonna waste it smooshing lips. Blech."

"How—do—you—figure?" Ellen grunted between breaths. She tried to keep the bite of irritation out of her tone, but Little Sister's pestering was getting—

"I *told* you. I fixed my time machine!"

Up in their shared bedroom, Ellen stood with her sore arms crossed and her foot tapping, but inside, her butterflies-turned-grasshoppers had made a second metamorphosis into bees. Bees of excitement.

Fixing the time machine, which had once caused the two of them a T. rex-sized problem—in that it had dropped them in the middle of the Cretaceous Period rather than either of the historical times they'd wanted to visit—had been a "side project" on Little Sister's science table for months now. Ellen had just about given up wondering if she'd ever get around to bringing the tangle of pipe cleaners and cardboard discs out of the prototype stage.

But if Little Sister was right and the time machine really was fixed, Ellen would have as much time as she wanted to perfect her party plans.

If she was willing to take the risk again of becoming Dino Dinner.

Little Sister grabbed the new model from the table, sent a pile of crayon-drawn schematics fluttering to the floor, and turned to present her handful to Ellen.

"Behold!" she said, sounding like a magician revealing her bag of tricks.

Ellen beheld, and was impressed. The time machine was no longer a mess of pipe cleaners, but instead a slick pink and mint green *Neko Hime* wristwatch with a few additions along the plastic band. Instead of one circle of cardboard serving as the dial, a series of four smaller cardboard pieces had been glued evenly spaced along the band. Each circle had a plastic jewel glitter glued in the center of it.

"The crystals are the piece I was missing before, as well as a more accurate timekeeper," Little Sister said as Ellen took the time machine and peered at it. "Those are placed in a precise array, which will stabilize the signal and allow us to arrive *exactly* When we mean to."

Ellen quirked an eyebrow. "And in normal-people-speak, that means?"

Little Sister rolled her eyes. "It means no more dinosaurs. Unless we *want* dinosaurs."

"I do not want dinosaurs," Ellen said automatically. Then she smiled. "But I do want time to make my party perfect."

"I've got a better idea. This new model is way more powerful than the prototype was." Little Sister's nose wrinkled as if thinking of her old failure had sent a whiff of spoiled milk under her nostrils. "It has plenty of juice to make two or even three round-trip jumps before it needs to recharge its power. I want to make *my* first jump to the end of the new year so I can see how things turn out before I make my resolutions tomorrow night. Why don't we also make a jump to January first so you can see how your party went before you plan it?"

Ellen blinked as she thought about this. Little Sister's logic made her head spin sometimes. But she thought she understood.

Go into the future for a peek, and she wouldn't have to *plan* her party. She could just see what she had chosen to do—would choose to do—and copy that.

It would be impossible *not* to impress Krista.

"Risako," she said, unable to stop her grin. "You're the most brilliant sister I could have asked for."

"Yes, I know," said Little Sister. But her matching grin kind of ruined the smug tone.

"What are we waiting for?" Ellen said.

Little Sister strapped the time machine around her own wrist, fiddled with the plastic band until it snapped snugly into place. Then she waved Ellen over.

Ellen stepped closer. She grabbed Little Sister's lab coat sleeve, digging her fingers into the rough fabric.

Little Sister lowered her goggles into place.

"Uh," said Ellen. "Should I have a pair, too?"

"Nah, just close your eyes."

A prickle of nervousness jarred through Ellen's buzzing excitement, but she shook it away. Little Sister was turning the dial on the wristwatch already. The tip of her tongue jutted out between her lips as she focused.

"Okay, here we go! We're jumping ahead exactly one year. Once I see what I will have managed to accomplish, I'll know what resolutions to make. Hold tight!"

Ellen gripped the sleeve so hard her knuckles turned white.

Little Sister clicked the dial into place.

Light flared, harsh and blue. Ellen hadn't closed her eyes yet, and she was instantly blinded, but she didn't dare lift her arm from Little Sister's to cover her eyes. A lurch from somewhere in her lower spine made her feel like she was about to be pulled off balance.

But all of that was normal when they used Little Sister's strange cardboard machines.

What wasn't normal was the icky, rotten-sweet, sticky taste of *natto*, of fermented soy beans, welling up in her mouth. Anything that tasted like that had to be going wrong.

"Little Sister," she tried to say. The words came out strange, somehow both slowed down and sped up. She felt like she was talking through bean-flavored syrup.

Through the gloop of time, Ellen thought she heard Risako's voice. "Eeeelllllleeen? Ln?"

The effect was starting to make her sick to her stomach. She didn't know how much longer she could handle it.

And then, with a teeth-clacking *thwump*, they fell out of the time gloop.

Ellen panted as if she'd just swum a million laps in the school pool. The air tasted clean, almost too clean. She swiped at her eyes, surprised her hands didn't come away covered in some slimy mess. Spots of light still danced in her vision, though, making it impossible to see anything. She could tell through feel that she knelt on a hard floor, probably metal. Beside and slightly behind her, Little Sister muttered like an angry astronaut.

"Risako! I'll tell Mom you said that."

"Ugh, I'm such an idiot!" Little Sister said. "I should have known these crystals were too powerful for the *Neko Hime* watch. They're all drained."

Ellen's heart sank at that. All her tummy butterflies-grasshoppers-bees were turning into tummy spiders. Their long legs sent shivers of *Danger! Danger!* up her spine.

"Risako..."

"Hi, girls!" came a cheerful voice. Someone was walking towards them. The sound of their footsteps was like a bird's toenails clicking on a kitchen floor. Ellen became aware of other voices around them, all murmuring like kids staring at someone who's just tripped in the cafeteria. In the distance, a robotic series of bleeps and bloops sequenced out some message. A motor whirred past, far overhead rather than along some nearby road.

Ellen blinked harder. Her vision still didn't clear. When she tried looking around, her head swam.

"Whoa now, looks like you've got a mild case of Time Sickness there," said the voice, coming lower as if the speaker had knelt beside her. They put a hand on her shoulder.

"T-Time Sickness?"

When *were* they?

"Sure thing. You should have worn some eye protection like your sister there. Don't worry, though! Here in the year 3999, we've got downloadable medicine for all the symptoms."

Ellen was too angry to care that she was arguing with Little Sister in front of their friendly guide.

"So much for the end of *one* year. Your stupid time machine blew us all the way to the end of the millennium. The *next* millennium!"

"I told you, it was an overflow of power from the jewels," said Little Sister, holding one of Ellen's arms as the three of them were whisked down the metal street by a car their guide had said ran on magnets. The seats were all made of some springy, foamy material, which smelled soothingly like green tea. The sound of the car was a soft, steady hum, and the motion was so gentle Ellen could barely feel it through her lingering dizziness.

Little Sister *sounded* like she was sorry. Ellen's eyes were still too full of sparkles for her to see if Little Sister wore a matching facial expression.

Ellen growled and rubbed her eyes again. "I've got *Time Sickness* because of your dumb jewels."

Risako mumbled some half-apology, but Ellen didn't listen. She knew the problem wasn't entirely Little Sister's fault, anyway. She knew she should have been more cautious about jumping to use the new time machine. Where had her Responsible Big Sister sense gone?

She knew where it had gone. She'd been too distracted thinking about getting Krista to kiss her at midnight. And where had it gotten her? Blown so far past the particular midnight in question it might as well never have happened!

Ellen didn't even know if she'd managed to earn a New Year's kiss at all.

"Well, girls," their guide chirped, bringing the car to a stop. "We're here! The Medicine Bank. They'll just connect your network chip to the system, and you'll be able to download the cure. Don't worry about which model chip you have. We get so many time travelers, they've seen it all, from the most primitive chip to ones even more sophisticated and advanced than ours."

"Uh," Ellen said. Her head was swimming again with the change in the car's speed. "I don't think I have a network chip?"

She felt Little Sister shaking her head next to her. "Nope. No chips."

The guide made a sound like a chicken coughing. "What? No chip? Impossible! Nobody's ever managed time travel without one. *Everyone* who comes to our time has some model of chip."

Little Sister huffed. She probably crossed her arms over her lab coat. "I don't work with weird tech like chips. They're too unreliable, and cardboard doesn't respond to them at all. I prefer to stick with my tried-and-true materials."

"Chips are the foundation of modern science," said the guide in a harder tone than they'd been using.

Ellen groaned. The last thing she needed while blind, dizzy, and heartsick was a battle of the scientists!

"Can I just get some of that medicine already?" she said.

"I'm sorry," said the guide. At least they'd returned to chipper and friendly. "But without a chip, the Medicine Bank will have no way of administering their cures. The only way to set you right again would be to return you to your proper time."

Ellen let her head fall back against the foamy head cushion. The green tea scent wafted over her, but it didn't do much to soothe her frustration. It reminded her too much of home, of Mom and Dad. They probably weren't around these days. Nobody she knew would still be around. Her school friends, her teachers, Krista...

Beside her, Little Sister spoke into her lap, turning the broken time machine over. "I don't know if I can find the materials I need in this time if everything is chip based. I need some new cardboard mounts for the jewels."

"Cardboard," clucked the guide. "Such primitive material. We don't keep it around. Magnetics are the wave of the future, you know. Our scientists jumped ahead a few years to see which technology they ought to invest their efforts in."

"Great," Ellen said.

But their guide laughed. "But this is the future to you two. We have all the time machines you need. We'll just run down to the Time Bank. What year are you from?"

The car picked up speed again, and Ellen swallowed against the wave of dizziness. They would get home just fine, she told herself. And then she could go back to planning her party down to the last detail. That midnight kiss would happen if it took spreadsheets and timetables to manage. She just had to hold on a little longer.

~

The Time Bank was a bustling place, full of future people coming and going. The sound inside was a deafening cacophony of ginormous clocks ticking, alarms ringing, and people shouting over it all to greet newcomers or wish happy travels on departures. As soon as Ellen shuffled in, clutching Little Sister's hand for balance, the scent of lemons and floor cleaner like her school used in the hallways assailed her nose. The floor squeaked under her shoes, and she guessed it was made of fancy marble—or the high-tech future equivalent.

Their guide led them through the throngs of people towards the nearest available Time Banker. "We'll simply have them access the ATM for your year, and before you know it, you'll be back in your own When feeling as good as new."

Someone brushed by Ellen's shoulder in a rush to get where he or she was going. Ellen gripped Little Sister harder to steady herself. "The ATM? Do we need cash to use the Time Bank?" She didn't have much in the savings account Mom and Dad had opened for her. Then again, she had just learned about how interest worked in her math class last week. Maybe she was a millionaire here in the future!

But the guide laughed. "Not an Automatic Teller Machine. ATM these days stands for Absolute Time Machine. Each machine is anchored to an exact—absolute—time, so it can reliably take you When you want to go and bring you back again if you want."

Little Sister pried Ellen's fingers from her arm. "Sounds inefficient. I'd much rather have a time machine that can take me to any time at all."

The guide made another coughing chicken sound but didn't have a chance to argue or explain further. They'd arrived at the counter, and a Time Banker was asking them how she might be of assistance.

"Hello, yes, my young friends here must return to their own time at once. Time Sickness, as you can see, and they *apparently* come from a When that doesn't use chips."

The Banker gasped like she was drowning. "*No* chips?"

"None whatsoever."

"How terrible! But we can help. What year do you need to access?"

The guide told her. The click-clack of the Banker tapping at buttons spilled from behind the counter, followed by a soft gasp of dismay. Ellen heard it like a crash over the hubbub of the rest of the Time Bank.

If only her stupid eyes worked! She opened them as wide as she could, but the sparkles danced as much as ever in her vision.

"I'm sorry," the Banker was saying. "It appears that year's account has been overdrafted. The ATM won't accept any more transactions."

"Hah!" said Little Sister. Ellen jumped at the unexpected burst of sound. "So your fancy tech doesn't work so well as you say after all."

Ellen turned to glare at her, ignoring both the fact she couldn't see if her glare was hitting right and the way the motion set her dizziness reeling. "Your scientific pride is *so* the least important part of this! We're stuck in the year 3999 unless this overdraft gets resolved or you fix *your* malfunctioning time machine! Not to mention I'll be blind and dizzy the whole time."

Oh man, what if she spent the rest of her life blind and dizzy?

Little Sister's shoulders slumped, making Ellen lean further over as her support slackened. "I'm just saying."

Dejected, Ellen and Little Sister tottered out of the Time

Bank. Their friendly guide paced beside them, squawking platitudes and empty comforts and telling them how lovely they would find living in the year 3999.

Ellen tried to tune them out. She had enough to focus on with fighting her spinning head at every step on this slippery floor. What a horrible New Year's Eve. She wanted to go home and spend the day with her friends and family, even if her party turned out a disaster.

Even if Krista Martin didn't want to kiss her at midnight, at least she'd be at the party.

"It'll all become second nature soon enough. You'll see," said the guide in a bright, feathery voice.

"I can't see *anything*," Ellen grumbled. "I'm blind."

"Right. Sorry."

The Time Bank's doors swept open on their wave-of-the-future magnets, and the three of them emerged onto the metal sidewalks.

"I want to go home," Ellen said.

"Me, too," Little Sister said, squeezing Ellen's hand. Then she perked up. "In fact, I think we *should* go home. Or at least to our house. I kept a stash of cardboard in our closet, you know."

Ellen tried to perk up herself, but her dizziness made it hard. "It's probably all rotted away by now."

"We won't know unless we look!"

Their guide spluttered. "But, it's New Year's Eve. This is a time for looking ahead, not into some primitive past. Surely you two will want to move forward with getting your chips installed and downloading all the latest ThoughtWare?"

Ellen flapped a hand instead of shaking her head. "I want to go home. But if you've got some special New Year's party to get to, we understand. Just point us to where we can get a map."

Little Sister made a sound of disappointment. "It would be

so interesting to gather data on what future New Year's Eve parties are like. I can't imagine what kinds of resolutions they make in 3999! But Ellen's right, we need to go home and work on fixing our time machine."

Their guide made the coughing chicken sound once again. Ellen was starting to wonder if their guide actually *was* part chicken. Did they make strange people-chicken cyborg creatures in the future? Maybe she should be glad she couldn't see anything but sparkles.

"New Year's parties? Resolutions? I have no idea what you two are talking about."

"You know," said Little Sister in her most insufferable explanatory tone. "A New Year's party where you and all your friends look back on the old year and make promises for what you'll do in the new year like 'I promise to do all my homework on time,' or 'I promise not to bother my big sister too much,' and the grown-ups stay up all night drinking out of fancy glasses and kissing someone at midnight."

Their guide made no response for a long moment, during which the magnetic whirring of cars passing them and the strange chatter of future people walking around them kept silence from descending. Ellen imagined the guide gaping at Little Sister, blinking their beady eyes in chickeny disbelief.

"That doesn't make any sense," said the guide at last. "Nobody's done any of those things on New Year's Eve since... well, since the year before the one you two come from."

"Oh, sure, we're the weirdos here," Little Sister said, mocking now. "Who needs parties or resolutions when you've got *chips* in your heads? Or was it magnets?"

Ellen clapped a hand over Little Sister's mouth. Well, she tried to. She got Risako's cheek, but it had the same quieting effect as covering her mouth would have done.

"There's no time for fighting! Don't you see, Risako? We

broke the time continuum coming here! Because we didn't have my party and you didn't make any resolutions, those things don't exist in the future!"

"So?"

Ellen gave her head a little shake, trying to tilt with her dizziness. Somehow, the way her head was spinning and her eyes were blinded helped her see their situation clearly. Even though the gloop of time ought to make no sense at all, she understood their paradox as if it were no more complex than first-grade addition and subtraction.

"So, the balances of the two times don't match. That's why the ATM account was overdrafted, and why we can't use it to get home. To fix the overdraft, we have to put parties and resolutions back into the year 3999."

Under her hand, Little Sister pouted. "That sounds like a lot of work. I'd rather just find some cardboard and—"

"There's no cardboard to find," Ellen said, gulping against a sudden surge of nerves. "We're going to have to do it the hard way. We're going to have to throw a New Year's Eve Resolution Making Party, and it has to go perfectly, or we're never getting back to our own time again. What time is it now?" she asked, turning to their guide.

"Precisely 5:38 in the afternoon."

The nerves swirled into a fresh swarm of unbalanced tummy butterflies, but she swallowed against them. "Okay, next question. Where's the nearest party store?"

Planning a party while suffering from constant dizziness and blindness was far more difficult than Ellen would have thought. Even harder was planning a party in an unfamiliar future apartment by explaining those plans to someone she suspected was half chicken.

"No, no, the snacks have to be set out on a table so everyone can help themselves throughout the night," she said from her perch on an egg-shaped future chair, trying to keep the exasperation from her voice. But she'd explained the arrangement of pretzel sticks and potato chips and three kinds of dip at least four times already. She wasn't sure she could handle the ordeal to come of tackling decorations.

At least their guide-turned-party-helper had decided they were intrigued by the idea of the Resolution Making New Year's Party. They'd eagerly offered their apartment as the site of the party and had sent off a flurry of invitations via the chip network. Ellen was doing her best to navigate the party space entirely by touch and smell. The temperature was pleasant enough, not too hot or cold, and the air tasted faintly like sunflower seeds and plastic. Not the most festive of scents, but it would have to do.

"But what happens when the sleep-cycle comes at 9:30?" they asked. "My friends don't understand that part. Is this a sleepover?"

"We don't sleep until after midnight. The whole point is to welcome in the New Year the moment it flips over. Did you put the drinks on their own table?"

"Yes, and the collection of fancy glasses, as you specified."

"Okay," Ellen said. She tapped her finger against her chin, thinking hard. What was she missing? Had she forgotten anything vital? Food and drink, check. Decorations, check, but still to be arranged properly. Party games? Time to check in with Little Sister on that one.

"How's the tree coming, Risako?"

Little Sister, as the one responsible for ensuring the resolutions went off properly, had come up with the brilliant idea of a

Resolution Tree. Partygoers could write out their resolutions on strips of paper, then tie them with a ribbon onto the boughs of a specially decorated tree, like perhaps a Christmas tree. It would help make the resolutions a real, tangible thing for a bunch of future people who had forgotten what resolutions were.

Little Sister's grunt came from the far corner of the room. "It's coming just great. Even if this paper is terrible quality."

"Good, good," Ellen said, already distracted with other plans. How could she communicate the layout of decorations to their guide when she couldn't even see the room she was decorating? How could she act as a good hostess when she could barely stand up without her head reeling with Time Sickness?

Before she could come up with an answer to either of those questions, a sharp, pecking knock came at the door, and her tummy butterflies started doing tummy loop-the-loops.

Their first guests had arrived.

The guide spoke a command to their chip, and the apartment door whirred open via the power of magnets. Instantly, a group of people entered, all chittering at once, their future shoes clicking against the metallic floor. The apartment filled with a cacophony like a flock of excited sparrows.

Ellen pushed at the plastic arms of her egg chair, about to rise to greet the guests, knowing she needed to make a good example of a New Year's party even if the decorations hadn't been hung yet, when a horrible realization smacked her right in the forehead.

"Oh no, I did forget something! The midnight kiss!"

Little Sister, having abandoned the Resolution Tree, shrugged. Ellen heard the lab coat shoulders rumple. "Eh, I wouldn't worry about it. We don't have to get every tradition right this time."

"But the kiss is the most important one," Ellen said. She was thinking of Krista Martin, and about all the careful plans she'd made for her real party back in her real time. "We have to make certain everything is in place so when midnight comes around people can find a good kissing partner, you know, someone you *want* to kiss, and hopefully she wants to kiss you, *too*, and—"

Little Sister's hand fell on Ellen's shoulder. Her grip was strong but reassuring. "Hey, don't worry about it. If people want to slobber all over each other's faces at midnight, they'll do it whether we've set the perfect atmosphere for it or not. It's not exactly a science, or so my research into the subject suggests."

Ellen let out a breath, and the butterflies in her tummy swirled. Could it be that simple? "I guess."

Another knock came at the apartment door, and after the magnetic hum, another flock of guests entered. The party space was getting quite noisy now, and warmer. Ellen fought against a wave of lightheadedness. She blinked hard one more time, but the bright flashes didn't dissipate. This party was the most important one she'd ever host. Even more important than her plans to impress Krista Martin.

And yet, now that the party sat on the cusp of starting, she felt calm. She might not have any idea how her careful—if hasty —planning would go over, but she realized now that the key piece of this party wasn't how meticulously it had been arranged, but that the guests themselves were present and eager to have a good time.

Little Sister was right. If their guests wanted to have a fun time at her party, they would, even without her fretting over every detail.

She hadn't even greeted anyone yet, and they were already making sounds like a party was in full swing!

Smiling, she raised her voice. "Is everyone ready to celebrate the New Year the old-fashioned way?"

The gathering answered with a chorus of *yes!*

Ellen squeezed Little Sister's hand, and Little Sister squeezed back.

They'd get out of this Time Jam together, just like they always did.

~

Ellen shook her head and blinked down at her bags full of subpar party supplies where they were slumped on the floor in the front room. Had she just fallen asleep on her feet? Maybe she'd been lulled by the piney scent of the Christmas decorations. And she'd had the strangest dream, as if she'd been suspended in gloop as she traveled through time...

A loud thump sounded from upstairs. It was followed by a sharp crash, a moment of heavy silence in which Ellen's heart had time to sink into the midst of the leaping grasshoppers in her tummy.

Grasshoppers? Right, because she was nervous about making her party perfect for Krista. Which was odd, because she knew the most important part of a party was how much fun everyone there wanted to have. She hoped Krista would want to kiss her at midnight, but even if they didn't kiss, Ellen would still be happy to see her at the party.

"I've *done* it!"

The rapid *thmp-thmp-thmp* of Risako's house slippers preceded her appearance on the stairs.

"Good, you're home. I mean, I knew you were home. I've *fixed* it!"

Ellen blinked up at Little Sister. Something about this felt weirdly familiar.

"You've... fixed your time machine," Ellen said, knowing she was right.

"Yes! And I've got a brilliant, amazing, impossible-to-fail idea—"

"Have we done this before?" Ellen interrupted.

"What? No, of course we—wait." Little Sister cocked her head, dragonfly goggles slipping out of place. "We have. Omigosh, it worked!"

Ellen opened her mouth, about to voice her certainty that the repaired time machine had *not* worked. Then she realized Little Sister wasn't talking about *that*.

"Our New Year's Eve Resolution Making Party must have balanced out the overdraft at the Time Bank," Ellen said. "And the ATM has sent us back to just a few moments before we made the jump."

She couldn't remember going to the Time Bank after the party. In fact, she couldn't remember staying awake until the end of the party. Still, her guests must have managed just fine without her guidance, as evidenced by the fact she stood here, in her own When, with nary a sparkle in her vision or a dizzy spell around her head.

Little Sister, still on the stairs, sighed. "Darn it. I didn't get to find out what I excelled at in the coming year, so I don't know what to do for my resolutions."

"But you did learn something," Ellen said. "You know those jewels won't work, so this time around you can save yourself the effort of testing them. Maybe you can direct your next attempt towards chips? Or maybe magnets!"

Little Sister stuck her tongue out at that. They both laughed.

"Besides, you're not supposed to know how your resolutions turn out, just like I shouldn't know ahead of time how my party is going to go. It ruins the fun if you know."

"Yeah, I guess so. Maybe the world isn't ready for time travel to the future. Oh! I know what I'll do for my resolution!"

"You promise not to bother your big sister too much?"

"No, I promise to perfect my time machine for *past* travel. It'll be dinosaurs all the time, anytime we want them!"

Ellen groaned. "Come on, Little Sister. Help me carry these party things down to the basement."

She didn't need any time machine to know she was exactly When she wanted to be, in the final hours of the old year, looking forward to whatever the New Year might bring.

About the Author

Brigid Collins is a fantasy and science fiction writer living in Nevada. Her fantasy series *The Songbird River Chronicles, Winter's Consort*, and *The Clockwork Kingdom Saga*, as well as her dark fairy tale novella *Thorn and Thimble* are available wherever books are sold. Her short stories have appeared in *Fiction River, Feyland Tales*, and Mercedes Lackey's *Valdemar* anthologies.

Want an extra Sugimori Sisters story? Sign up for her newsletter at www.brigidcollinsbooks.com/newsletter-sign-up/ and get a free copy of *Strength & Chaos, Mischief & Poise: Four Cat Tales*, exclusively available to her subscribers!

Support Brigid on Patreon! Featuring monthly short stories, blog posts, and behind-the-scenes tidbits in a pay-what-you-want structure. Come hang out! patreon.com/BrigidCollins